CHRISTMAS IN CYPRESSVILLE

CYPRESSVILLE SMALL TOWN ROMANCE

KRISTEN TASSIN

TASTEC INK

ISBN 978-1-7374589-0-6 eBook

ISBN: 9798325280955 Paperback 2nd Edition

ISBN 978-1-7374589-1-3 Paperback 1st Edition

Developmental Editor- Tina Canon

Editor- Shona McLaren

Proofreader- Nathan Winfrey

Cover Design- KTK Design

To my mom and dad who encouraged me to dream.

CHRISTMAS IN CYPRESSVILLE

CHAPTER ONE

$\mathcal{M}$elissa Albright walked out of Main Street Java to her phone's text alerts going wild. Taking a sip of her latte, she looked through the front window of the coffee shop. Walter had one of his employees spray it with fake snow, attempting to make their Southern town look like it had a white Christmas. To add more holly jolly cheer, they added green garland and blinking lights. She rolled her eyes and groaned as she left the cafe.

Melissa walked farther down the street. Someone had placed a giant inflatable snowman surrounded by equally large ornaments in the center of the traffic circle for display. It was more than she could handle. If it were her, she would have gone with something a little less inflatable and a little more sophisticated.

"Don't go there," she muttered. She breathed a sigh of relief when a lovely bare brick wall became visible. After her mom passed away, her life slowly went downhill. Melissa's heart ached on so many levels that the season's love and joy stifled her. Since Thanksgiving, she had been secluding herself inside her house, trying to avoid the season at all costs.

If her mom had been there, she might not have had to move back in with her dad after last Christmas's work fiasco. Her mom had a way of turning something embarrassing into something she could laugh about. But she couldn't find anything funny about her career going down the drain. Although, moving home did have some perks. She started writing again, something she hadn't done since high school. And best of all, her dad's fiancée gifted her a rescued Yorkie puppy named Snickerdoodle.

Melissa brought Snickerdoodle with her everywhere. She opened her doggie tote bag and pulled Snickerdoodle out, feeding her a Puppuccino. Putting her on her leash, they walked across the street to a small park before heading over to her friend Jenna's shop. She pulled her phone out of her pocket to read Jenna's messages.

I hope you got my triple espresso!

I'm in serious need.

I'm dying. Where are you?

I stayed up all night with my nephew.

Me babysitting! For a week!

What was I thinking when I said Yes!

What was Lee Anne thinking when she asked? He cried all night.

Good thing I'm not married FYI- I'm not ready for kids.

Hurry! The machines are lulling me to sleep.

ZZZZZZZZZZZZ

Melissa couldn't help but laugh out loud at the rest of the messages sent a couple of minutes later. Jenna must have felt Melissa's morose vibes from down the street in the monogram shop. She was texting in single words like they used to in high school.

When

Are

You

Coming!

Can't

Hold

Back

Any

Longer

I

Have

Juicy

Gossip!!!

OMG

A cool breeze fluttered her hair into her eyes. Tucking the flyaway strand behind her ear, she was reminded of how good to it felt to be outside. Today was the first time in weeks Melissa stepped away from her computer. After being rejected by over twenty literary agents, one was kind enough to give her a critique, telling her that her ideas were good, but she needed to find the characters' voices. She said they were flat. Since then,

Melissa had been hyper-focused on her rewrites, but Jenna wasn't about to let her resume hibernation without a visit. Plus, Melissa hoped to get Jenna to run a couple of errands with her.

The mayor, Andrea, who was also her Dad's fiancée, asked Melissa if she wouldn't mind helping her buy gifts for the influencers attending the town's Christmas tree lighting. But she didn't trust herself to pick out the most appropriate gifts for them. Nor did she desire to do anything Christmas related, and her entire attitude felt somewhat grinch-like since Thanksgiving. Her typically charitable heart was at an all-time low.

The fact that she'd have to plant a fake smile on all night at the Christmas tree lighting designed to entertain influencers was bad enough. She hoped her attitude would change before then, and she didn't want to pretend to be cheerful for her dad's wedding that would take place immediately after. That thought alone made her stomach churn with guilt. It was a nightmare, and Melissa worried about how she'd get through the wedding. She loved Andrea, but she was completely different from her mother.

Melissa's heart couldn't figure out what it felt. Some moments it was happy for her dad. Others were like her current mood, sad that her dad moved on so quickly. Her eyes burned as they filled with tears. She glanced at the passersby. Melissa wouldn't cry in public. She blinked rapidly, preventing the tears from escaping.

Melissa pulled the leash loop over her wrist, pulled a Kleenex out of her pocket, and wiped the tears that decided to escape against her wishes. The last words her mom told her were, "If your dad finds love again, I will be okay with it. I want you both to keep the walls down and find love. It's the greatest gift of all, and you need it to thrive."

It was hard to want what her mother wanted. She couldn't help but protect her heart, shattered long ago by someone who didn't even know it. And now her dad found love twice. He'd only known Andrea a few weeks before they were serious. How could they form such a strong bond so soon? It couldn't be possible.

It's not that Melissa didn't like Andrea—she did, and she was grateful Andrea brought her dad out of mourning. But sometimes, she wondered if her dad had loved her mom as much as she thought. How could he fall in love only a year after losing the love of his life?

Maybe lasting love isn't what she imagined true love to be. Perhaps it was all about timing. Melissa and her ex-boyfriend Paul's relationship fizzled out after leaving her high-profile job as an event planner, and she never once looked back to her old life. That wasn't a lasting love unless you considered six years lasting. What exactly did her mother mean?

Melissa blew her bangs out of her eyes, frustrated at where her mind was taking her this morning.

She returned to her phone to reply to Jenna's messages. Her ringtone blared out "Carol of the Bells," and she groaned. Her dad snuck behind her back again for the third time this season and changed the tone on her phone to her once-favorite Christmas carol, trying to get her in the mood. It failed. She cleared her throat and put on her fake cheery voice, the one she used for clients.

"Hey, Dad!"

"Morning, Sugarplum!" His false cheeriness forced Melissa's shoulders to tense.

Her tone immediately changed to one of dread. "Oh, no! What did you do?"

"What do you mean?" His voice hitched a pitch higher, something he did whenever he had upsetting news. Melissa learned this new tell this year living with him. The first time was when he started dating the mayor after helping her with her campaign. The most recent was when Walter from the coffee shop congratulated her on her dad's proposal. She had to confront him, hurt that she found out second hand.

"You only call me Sugarplum these days when you're up to something. What is it this time?"

"Well..."

The coffee turned sour in her stomach. "Spit it out, Dad."

The phone disconnected. As Melissa was about to call her dad back, she noticed him jogging across the street toward her. At fifty-five she admired how her dad kept in better shape than she did.

She waved, picked Snickerdoodle up, and held her in her arms, ready to greet her dad.

"Hey Dad, I didn't know you'd be in town today."

Her dad gave her a one-armed hug, then gave Snickerdoodle a little love. "Andrea had a bit of a crisis this morning. I just left her office."

He wiped his hands on his pants as if his palms were sweating. Although winters were warm down south, it wasn't that hot. She knew whatever he was about to say wasn't good, and Melissa mentally tried to prepare herself.

"What happened?"

"You know how this is Andrea's first term as mayor?"

She nodded and waited for him to go on. This couldn't be good. Her dad started pacing with his hand rubbing the back of his neck. Her heart began to race in anticipation of what he would say. The seconds of silence felt like days, and she couldn't wait any longer and urged him along.

"Dad?"

"Sugarplum, you're going to have to forgive me."

Melissa closed her eyes, took a deep breath, and rolled her neck, cracking it. When she opened her eyes, her dad wouldn't face her. He was now sitting on the bench with his head in his hands. "What did you do?"

She held Snickerdoodle close to her chest for comfort and sat on the bench beside her dad. He finally looked up.

"Andrea kept it together at City Hall, but once we were alone in her office, she broke down in tears in my arms."

Although Melissa worried her dad and Andrea were rushing to get married, she really cared for her. She admired her strength and independence, and she hated hearing that a powerful woman like Andrea could break.

"Is she okay now? What happened?"

"The event planner she hired for our wedding and the tree lighting at the winter festival eloped and is on a plane to Cancún."

"That's horrible!"

"It is. She was beside herself. Not only is she concerned about the economy of the town, the influencers will begin arriving in less than twenty-four hours, days earlier than we expected. And now she doesn't have anyone to coordinate the most important event of her life."

"That sucks." Melissa felt heartless with that bland comment, but her shoulders fell in relief when that was all that was wrong. She thought Andrea had been sick or injured. Losing an event planner in the grand scheme of things was nothing. She couldn't find it in herself to be more upset. She tried to emote more feeling in her tone to give her dad the impression she wasn't totally cold-hearted.

"But I don't understand what that has to do with me forgiving you?"

There was a long pause. Melissa became impatient, shifted to hold Snickerdoodle with one arm, and the other hand made circular motions encouraging him to answer. "…And?"

"Well, clients used to fight over you back when you planned events. You could do this in your sleep. Compared to all the events you planned in the past, Cypressville's small festival would be a piece of cake. After all, you're a genius at organizing and making something simple into simply beautiful."

A smile graced her lips momentarily at his praises, then she frowned. It was her mom who encouraged and inspired her while she was an event planner. She lost her ability when her mom got sick, and the last event she planned right before her mom passed was the start of her downfall. By the end of the year, Melissa thought she was finally back on track when she landed the biggest job of her career. She was wrong. The Advocate newspaper immortalized the entire debacle of an evening on the front page as the worst social event of the season:

Perfect Planning Isn't So Perfect

The Winter Ball's hundred-year celebration was destroyed in a single moment when Melissa Albright from Perfect Planning created the devastating social faux pas of the century, seating the Governor next to his mistress rather than his wife.

Melissa shivered at the memory. All those people's shocked faces. She didn't know the woman was on the invite list, and his wife was understandably furious. That wasn't the worst part. She had the entire event planned to serve meat and found out that night that the governor's wife had explicitly requested the menu be vegan. How had it gone so wrong? Event planning had been the perfect job until that night.

Melissa adored parties but never wanted to be part of them. She had been a wallflower her entire life. Event planning was the best of both worlds. She could experience the event and remain invisible. She thrived behind the scenes, and the reward was watching others enjoy what she created and put together. In the four years since she finished college, she had succeeded, or so she thought, until that horrible night.

At that particular event, she somehow ended up being the focus. The entire night was a blur in her memories. Shock and devastation pushed her over the edge, and her boss finally sent her home on a sabbatical to grieve and disappear while her boss fixed the mess Melissa caused. She never went back to the city or her job. She couldn't. It hurt too much.

"I left that behind," Melissa told her dad. "I'm a writer now."

"Yeah, yeah, I know, but as I was comforting her, it popped out of my mouth without thinking."

"What exactly popped out of your mouth?"

"That you would gladly take over the festival, the Christmas tree lighting, and planning our wedding."

Her mouth went dry. "Dad, you have to be kidding me."

"I'm sorry." He sounded contrite, his voice sped up, panicked. "I can't take it back now. You should have seen Andrea's face light up. If you could have seen how heartbroken she was when she arrived, I know you would have volunteered yourself." He sounded as if he believed his words.

Melissa tilted her head back, face up toward the sun, and inhaled a deep breath.

"Mel, if the influencers weren't arriving for the festival and our wedding, I wouldn't have put you in this position. Our town, Andrea, is depending on this. We need the publicity to help bring in tourism. Plus, I love Andrea, and I want her wedding to be as perfect as she is imagining."

They remained silent for a few tense moments.

Her dad grabbed her hand, forcing the irritation to subside. His warmth seeped into her chilled hand. "Sugarplum, I really can't watch Andrea cry. Keeping the town from bankruptcy—"

Melissa interrupted her dad. Her heart stuttered in shock. "Is Cypressville bankrupt?"

He sighed. "It hasn't been good for a long while. Andrea has been doing everything in her power to make things turn around, and this festival is our big opportunity. To add to her stress, she wanted our wedding moved up earlier to be the night of the tree lighting, hoping to create a romantic ambiance and encourage others to consider having destination weddings with a small-town Southern charm."

"I had no idea all this was going on. Why haven't y'all talked to me about this?"

"Andrea didn't want to bother you. She knew you left the industry, plus you've been locked into writing since you moved back home. It never was really the right time to talk about it."

The conversation paused. Melissa sat contemplating her dad's words.

Her dad spoke once more when he realized she wasn't going to remark. "Andrea believes that we are guaranteed an increased revenue because of the influencers. Each one she hired has helped change many other small towns with their advertising. This is our last hope to bring our town back. She wanted everything to be perfect, especially our wedding. The final blow was discovering that the event planner took the deposit she was given to elope. I had to help, and it came in the form of you."

"Dad, this is already so hard. It's not my favorite time of the year. You know what happened last time I planned a Christmas event. How do you expect me to pull this off in…" She mentally counted in her head, then turned to her dad wide-eyed and said anxiously, "Five days! How can I save the economy of

Cypressville? I can't fail you and Andrea or our town. This is a lot to ask."

"You are too hard on yourself, Mel. That one event is not a reflection of your entire career. Plus, your boss Diane explained it was her ex-boyfriend trying to get back at her, you need to stop taking the blame. She even had the Advocate retract the article with an apology letter. Not to mention all of the further articles written about the lawsuit between him and the governor proved you were not at fault, nor was the company you worked with."

The apology letter was on page ten in a small corner of the paper's social section. Few people would have seen it. By the time Melissa's boss had it all fixed, Melissa felt as if the Advocate already dragged her name through the mud, and no one would want to hire her to plan their events ever again. She was angry and humiliated, but worst of all any good event planner checked and double checked everything. She got lax.

But this event wasn't for hire. It was for family. Melissa's heart palpitated in her chest harder as she considered her dad's words. "When I worked in the city, I had a team. There is no team here."

Her dad's voice cheered up now that Melissa was talking about it. Before she stopped him, he rushed onward. "Don't worry. We'll find you volunteers. The entire town wants this to succeed. I'm sure once we talk to all the Main Street shop owners, you will have plenty of help. Andrea told me she put a call in for her previous assistant, Susan. She recently quit and is opening a new gift shop on Main. Andrea is hoping she will be your right hand. I'm sure Jenna will be on board and Walter at the cafe."

Snickerdoodle barked at the name. Melissa pulled out a small treat Walter made especially for the puppy. The little

Yorkie nibbled the snack out of Melissa's palm as her dad rambled animatedly about who he'd talk to help her out.

Snickerdoodle finished the cookie, licking Melissa's fingers, making her give the animal her first genuine smile of the day. She loved that little dog. Snickerdoodle held the most beneficial role in her healing; she filled the void of love missing inside Melissa. It was unconditional. Melissa kissed Snickerdoodle on the head and placed her gently in the puppy tote.

Melissa stood, picked up the coffee carrier with Jenna's now cold triple shot. "Look, Dad, I need to go. No promises, but I'll think about it. I'm on my way to see Jenna, and I'll pass the idea by her."

He got up and gave Melissa another half hug. "Thanks, Melissa. You'll do the right thing. Love you."

Melissa wanted to say something sarcastic about him laying the guilt on thick but stuck with, "Love you too."

CHAPTER TWO

Ity maintenance crews were out winding garland up
every lamppost and stringing the lights across the
road. When evening approached, the cars driving down
Main Street would go through a tunnel of lights. Melissa
walked farther down the street on her way to Jenna's store,
mentally scratching decorations off the list. She stopped in
her tracks and groaned, realizing that she was probably
grudgingly going to do it.

With the coffee carrier in hand, she entered Jenna's shop.
The door dinged. Melissa barely entered the store before
Jenna, threading the monogram machine, hollered out "Welcome!" without looking up. Melissa walked in between boxes
scattered around the entryway. A bare tree stood in the
window awaiting its decorations. Melissa said a silent prayer,
hoping she wouldn't be asked to help decorate the thing.

"Hey, Jenna. I come bearing gifts," Melissa reciprocated

Jenna looked up with a big smile gracing her lips. "Mel,
thank goodness you finally made it. What took so long?"

"I ran into Dad at the park. Sorry, your coffee's cold."

Jenna grabbed her espresso from Melissa, walked to the

back of the shop, placed the coffee in the microwave, and heated it up.

She came back up front and hopped up on her counter to sit. "It's been too long since we hung out. I'm glad you made time to stop by and visit me at work, especially since you bailed on me—how many times now?"

"Yeah." Melissa wanted to tell her it had nothing to do with her and was all about not wanting to have any reminders of Christmas, but she didn't and went on with her preconceived excuse. "I know, but ever since I actually got some feedback on my book, I've been frantic to finish it. I totally get what the agent was saying now."

Snickerdoodle chose that moment to bark and make herself known.

"Did your purse just bark?" Jenna laughed.

Melissa reached into her bag, pulled out a wagging Snickerdoodle, and held her close to her face. "Snickerdoodle, this is Jenna, Jenna, Snickerdoodle." The dog yapped happily in greeting, and both women laughed.

"When did you get a dog?" A burst of laughter rushed out of Jenna in a "bahaha" sound. "The dog literally has the same hair color as you."

"Andrea rescued her a few months back and gave her to me. Snickerdoodle is a sweetheart, aren't you, baby?" Melissa gave the dog three loud smooches on her head, and the Yorkie excitedly licked her back.

"How long have you two been an item?" Jenna laughed goodnaturedly.

Melissa smiled. "I missed your wit."

"Baloney, now tell me the truth. What dragged you out of your dungeon?"

Melissa gave Jenna a fake frown. "I miss hanging out with you. Isn't that enough?"

"It would be if it were true."

"Can I let Snickerdoodle explore?"

"Sure, as long as she doesn't pee on my floors."

Melissa put Snickerdoodle down. "I was originally hoping you'd come shopping with me. I need to buy some thank you gifts for the influencers coming into town for the festival. But now it's even worse."

Jenna jumped off the counter at Melissa's sullen expression. "What's going on?"

"Dad volunteered me to be the event planner for the festival and his wedding."

Jenna just stared at Melissa, gauging her facial expression for a few seconds before speaking. "Why and what did you tell him?"

Melissa's body deflated. "Her event planner bailed to elope in Cancún, all expenses paid with Andrea's deposit money."

"Dang, that's harsh."

"Agreed." Melissa, like her dad, paced when she had something uncomfortable to say. "I feel bad. I was pretty cold about it to him. I have zero desire to help, and honestly don't think I can put myself in that line of fire again, especially after what happened last year. Dad doesn't get it, and I don't want to explain it to him. He believes that it was just that one event; it's hard to explain. It started long before that dreadful night. My inspiration has completely gone. It left with Mom."

Jenna looked on with a sympathetic expression. "So, did you tell him no? I bet that devastated him. He probably thinks you don't want him to marry Mayor Jackson."

"Oh, no, he has to know that isn't it. I didn't flat out say no—I told him I'd think about it."

Jenna's eyes widened, and a wide grin graced her lips.

Melissa rolled her eyes. "Don't get too excited. I didn't agree yet, and regardless of whether I do or not, they'll be contacting all Main Street owners to pitch in and help."

"You can count me in as long as it doesn't interfere with my helping take care of Andrew." Jenna sighed. "He's with me another few days and in daycare till six PM, and if he can be with me after hours to help, then I will be all hands on deck."

Melissa sighed in relief, knowing Jenna would be there for her. "Thanks, but to make matters worse, he also dropped the bomb that the town might be going bankrupt. And the entire town is depending on this festival being a success to help increase sales and bring in more business from surrounding areas."

Jenna shook her head in a knowing way. She probably had already heard or figured that out. She had a way of finding things out before anyone else. "I can't believe Mayor Jackson got the influencers to come to our little town. I started following them on Instagram the moment I heard, and some of them are no joke. Every place they go to seems to help increase sales. It'll sure help put us on the map."

"I know."

Jenna put her arm around Melissa in comfort. "Whatever you decide, I got your back."

Melissa gave Jenna a half hug. "Thanks. Now tell me this gossip you texted about earlier."

Even though Jenna was twenty-seven, she started jumping up and down. Once again reminding Melissa of when they were both teens in high school.

"You will never guess who is back in town."

Melissa's curiosity was up. "Who?"

"Jake Blessing!"

CHAPTER THREE

*J*ake walked down the stairs and entered the bright kitchen of his childhood home. It hardly changed at all since he moved out nearly ten years ago. His sister, Susan, bought it from their parents when they decided to spend their retirement traveling the states in an RV. Her divorce and their decision coincided, making the sale much easier for his parents, knowing they'd always have a place to come back home to. He watched her from the entry as she puttered around the stove. Susan was in week three of her recovery from ankle surgery.

If humming Christmas carols as she stirred batter was any indication, she looked to be on the upswing this morning. Secretly he was glad she woke up ready to do the cooking. His cooking lacked imagination and skill, and it hadn't taken her long to get tired of it. She complained so much about it that he started ordering every meal out after day four, so much so that he should buy stock in Main Street Java and Cypressville Diner.

"What are you doing on both feet? The doctor said no pressure on your ankle for another week."

She jumped at his voice but didn't turn around toward him and immediately propped her knee back on the medical knee scooter he rented to help her get around the house.

"Geez, little brother, you're as bad as my physical therapist. I should have called Mom back from their travels to help me out instead of you. She'd understand the need to move around the kitchen without this thing." She tried to bring the knee scooter closer to the stove. Reaching over the thing, she awkwardly flipped the pancakes on the griddle.

"Go set the table and be useful, please."

Jake pulled the plates out of the cabinet and set to work.

These past few weeks back in Cypressville he discovered how much his family meant to him. He enjoyed the small town's slower pace and the friendships he developed with some Main Street merchants. Jake started to wonder if he could become a freelance editor and move back home rather than returning to the city and his job at the small publishing company his friend Ben ran.

After Molly died, he practically ran away and blocked out his entire family. It had been four years since he'd been back. A sad smile crossed his lips at the lost time. Four years since he'd seen Molly's smile. She used to pick on him for always wanting to come back to Cypressville after college. He hadn't thought of her in a long while. He rubbed the sudden ache in his heart at this realization. The first year he put all his energy into work and made excuse after excuse to avoid coming home.

His biggest fear coming back was being reminded of Molly all over town, but that fear was wasted. The new mayor changed so much of the downtown this past year with her regeneration plan. He barely recognized his hometown. Despite it all, he loved the painted mural, tree-lined streets, and the modern vibe she brought to the storefronts in the center of town.

He also learned Molly's family moved away two years ago. Another moment of melancholy surfaced, knowing he purposely lost touch with them. But it was better this way. They could also move on. The only thing he worried about now was the

Christmas festival. It started this week, and the tree lighting was Saturday. The thought of having to go would be the next step to putting his past to rest.

It was the event where he asked Molly to be his steady girlfriend all those years ago. His first semester of college. He had missed her so much and wanted her to move with him. The following May, when she graduated from high school, they got married. Everyone thought they were crazy to get married so young, but they both wanted to be together. Looking back, he was grateful they did. Fate knew she'd be taken from this earth early on. The memories no longer hurt, and hopefully going to the festival would bring his healing full circle. He was ready to come home.

He went to help Susan bring the pancakes to the table.

Susan turned around and made a startled yelp. "Why do you always sneak up behind me?"

"Because it wouldn't be a good morning if I didn't." Jake stole a piece of bacon off a dish beside the stove and chuckled.

Susan glared at him playfully, then threw her oven mitt in his face.

"Hey now." He tutted with a grin.

She rolled her eyes. He picked up the serving plates loaded with breakfast foods.

"You might complain about having to use that knee scooter, but as I see it, you seemed to figure out how to maneuver around the kitchen pretty quick. I'm starting to wonder if I'm needed anymore."

He gave Susan a pouty face then turned around quickly,

making a ring-ring sound. "What is that I hear?" He answered an imaginary phone. "Work's calling. Your shop is sick of me and ready for you to come back," he joked.

"You've only been here for a few weeks, and you're already trying to leave. Thanks a lot, little brother." They both laughed. "Actually, I had to learn to use this knee walker on wheels because Megan and I were sick of your cooking. One can only handle so many slices of burnt toast and rubbery eggs."

"Harsh." Jake smiled, taking the insult with grace. She acted like she was joking, but there was sure to be a ring of truth to her statement. He rarely cooked. Being alone, he ate out most meals, and his cooking was lacking.

Susan pointed to the cabinet now wrapped in gift wrap and a bow. "Can you grab the napkins stored on the top shelf and refill my dispenser? If you do, I'll give you some breakfast."

"You made enough for an army, there's no need to try and bribe me." He got up to do as ordered. He grimaced, looking at the horrendous cabinets. Susan and her daughter insisted Christmas wouldn't be the same if he didn't do his share of the decorating. So, as the good brother and uncle, he grudgingly wrapped the kitchen cabinets with old seventies psychedelic wrapping paper and bows he found in the attic.

The wall clock chimed seven. Susan started muttering something under her breath.

"Sue, everything okay?"

"Yeah, just moving slower than I'd like. Can you see if Megan is almost ready for school? I hate that I still can't go up and down the stairs, and I don't want her to miss breakfast again. That girl's head has been in the clouds since you got into town."

Megan was in her room playing with her dolls. "Why yes, miss, I promise when the festival lights go on, I will give you true love's kiss."

Jake had to cover his mouth with his hand not to laugh at his little niece's playing. He wondered where she came up with half the things she imagined at only five years old. Before he had to witness the dolls' kiss, he knocked on the open door.

"Megan, what are you doing? You're supposed to be getting ready for school."

Megan jumped. Her guilty expression immediately disappeared when her uncle smiled. Megan got up and ran to him, hugging his leg. She quickly backed away and twirled in her dress.

"I am dressed. I had extra time, so I took advantage of it."

"What?" His eyes widened, and his mouth dropped slightly open, amazed a five-year-old would say something like that.

Her smile faded, and her voice became small. "It's what you told Momma yesterday when she caught you playing a video game instead of working?"

He laughed and ruffled the hair on her head. "I guess you're right. We all need to seize the day whenever we can."

She repeated his words questioningly, "Seize the day? What does that mean?"

"It means we need to make the most out of our day and take hold of something wonderful and enjoy it."

Her eyes widened, and she ran back to her dolls and picked up the Ken doll. "Mr. Doll seized the day and told his girlfriend he would kiss her at the light festival."

Jake laughed. "So he did." He held his hand out to Megan, "Come on, let me fix your hair before your mom fusses at me."

He made a few passes with the brush. "Good enough, your mom has breakfast ready. And we both need to seize the day. She made our favorite butter pecan pancakes with caramel and chocolate drizzle."

The delight that entered her eyes was contagious. She grabbed his hand excitedly, pulling him behind her down the stairs.

"Hurry, Uncle Jake, I have to eat a whole stack, and that takes a while."

The thought about moving home entered his mind again. Could he really make the change?

The constant activity surrounding Susan and Megan made him realize how dull his life was in the city and how working to exhaustion, eating, sleeping, and repeating had lost its appeal.

Jake brought the food to the table while Susan used her scooter to get to her seat. Megan sat down, bouncing in her chair in anticipation of her breakfast. He didn't even realize how empty and alone he'd become. Disgust washed over him, thinking of how he abandoned his family out of his initial grief, which became a daily habit. How long would it have taken him to return if his sister hadn't needed him?

He shook away those morose thoughts and listened to Megan chattering away happily to her mom. When a moment of silence came, Susan turned to Jake. "I got a call from Mayor Jackson while y'all were upstairs."

"What did she have to say? Is she missing her favorite employee now that you left to open your shop?"

"Of course. Who wouldn't miss me?" She winked at Megan. "There's a bit of an issue. Her event planner eloped and is in Cancún as we speak. She asked if I could be the new planner's assistant once they find a replacement."

"What did you tell her?" he asked innocently before taking a bite of his pancake.

"Well..." She drew out the word.

Jake placed his fork on the table, wiped his hands, and looked at Susan with suspicion. Her face paled, and she chuckled nervously and repeated the same word with a squeak to her voice.

"Susan, what did you say? Please don't tell me you volunteered me."

Guilt was written all over Susan's face. She wouldn't look at Jake, preoccupying herself with picking up her plate awkwardly and attempting to bring it with her scooter to the kitchen. Jake got up, rounded the table, and roughly took it out of her hands and set it in the sink.

Susan spoke softly. "Before I quit, I promised both Elise and the mayor that I'd help with the festival, but when I had the accident and had to have surgery, Elise told me that she'd take me off the list and tell Andrea, but obviously, she forgot."

Jake cleared the rest of the table, picking up the plates a bit aggressively, nearly knocking over Megan's half-full milk glass. Megan caught it before it toppled over, watching her mom and uncle bicker.

"Call Mayor Jackson back and tell her I will not submit myself to party planning. I'm busy enough as it is helping you open the store. The grand opening is Thursday, and nothing is on the shelves yet. How do you expect me to find the time to assist a party planner?"

"I can't tell the mayor no. She didn't know I had surgery and was upset I didn't tell her sooner. I swear Andrea sounded like she was near tears. It just accidentally came out of my mouth that you were in town helping me out, and when she told me that Melissa Albright was possibly taking Elise's place, I figured—"

Jake cut her off. "Geez, seriously. I can't believe this."

He threw the towel on the counter. He paced with his hands on his hips for a few seconds, then took a deep breath and blew it out. "I need to go for a walk."

Before he made it to the door, Susan shouted from the kitchen, making her way to meet him. "Jake, please don't be mad."

"I'll be fine. I just need some air."

Megan ran outside, trying to catch up. "Uncle Jake, wait up!"

"Megan, you can't come with me. You need to wait for the bus."

Megan ignored him, grabbed his hand, and kept walking with him until he stopped. He sighed and turned back, making his way back to their Acadian-style house. They waited at the end of the driveway for the bus.

They stood quietly for a whole two seconds before Megan started prattling. "Why are you so mad? Who is Melissa Albright? Why aren't you seizing the day?"

The roar of the bus marked its arrival. It stopped in front of the house, and the doors folded open. Jake muttered under his breath. "Saved by the bus."

He laid his hand on Megan's back, guiding her to the bus. "Have a good day at school, kiddo."

"Aww, Uncle Jake, you have to tell me," Megan whined, climbing the steps into the bus.

"Another day, princess."

CHAPTER FOUR

Jake ended up walking a quarter of a mile into town. He wasn't aware Melissa was back. "Of course, she'd come back," he muttered. The knowledge of her dad being the mayor's fiancé had evaded his mind. Out of habit, he walked into Main Street Java. By the time he realized and was about to turn around to leave, Walter had already spotted him.

He called out to him from the register. "Morning, Jake. The usual?"

Embarrassed to admit the blunder, he caved and placed his order. "Yes, sir. How's your knee doing?"

"Fine, getting old is for the birds. The things that used to be so easy are a bit harder these days. My mind tells me I'm capable, but my body says the opposite."

"If you need me for anything involving ladder climbing again, I'd be more than happy to help."

Walter rolled his eyes. "I'm not a baby, son. I can still climb a ladder." He sighed, looked up at the high ceilings, and limped to make the coffee.

When he returned, his voice sounded as if he'd conceded

he might need help. "I appreciate the offer and could use your help to add some more lights if you're free."

Jake grabbed the Americano and his everything bagel with cream cheese off the counter, then gave a two-finger salute to Walter. "I'll be here at closing time."

"Thank you," Walter said as Jake turned to leave, nearly running into Jenna Thorne.

"Jake!" Jenna's eyes widened. "I haven't seen you in ages. Are you visiting Susan?"

"Yeah, I'm helping her with the grand opening. She had to have surgery on her foot and wouldn't have been able to open in time for the festival."

"Oh wow, I hadn't heard. I sure would have brought her a casserole."

"You know Susan never wants to put anyone out. I'm surprised she kept it quiet this long."

"Well, it won't be quiet long. You had to tell the town blabbermouth."

They both laughed.

He joked, "Just remember you said it, not me."

"I hate to say it, but I can't deny it anymore. I always get caught, and everyone knows if they don't want something to spread, don't tell me." Jenna started toward the counter to place her order. "It was good to see you."

"Same to you." Jake started walking away, hesitated, then turned back to Jenna, wanting to confirm what Susan told him. "Is Melissa in town?"

Jenna turned around quickly, her eyes wide, and smiled mischievously. "She moved back last December. She gave up event planning and is writing full-time. Are you planning on looking her up?"

"No, I was just curious." Jake hurried out without another word. He felt like sticking his foot in his mouth when the sound of Jenna giggling reached his ears. What had he done?

He should have kept his mouth shut. Jenna was probably on the phone calling Melissa right now, telling her he was in town.

Melissa was a fantastic friend back in high school, the best, actually. They practically were inseparable since they first partnered up in class. Since he left home, he found himself missing her friendship. Even Molly used to bring her up occasionally, telling him he should call her. He almost called her for the first time since high school last year to see if she was okay after that horrible newspaper article slammed her planning event but decided against it, thinking she wouldn't react well, being they hadn't spoken in years.

But there was never anything between them besides friendship. Why was he even dwelling on this? Melissa being in town was irrelevant. He was here to help his sister with the grand opening for the Christmas festival, not rekindle his friendship with a girl who quit being his friend when he started dating Molly. She wasn't worth the effort thinking about. What friend ditches you?

Frustrated, he speed-walked through the busy sidewalks to get to his sister's shop.

On his walk to Susan's shop, he noticed that shop owners were working on their window displays and storefronts, trying to up their ante with the decorations this year. He was sure Susan would be asking him to do the same to her storefront as well to keep up appearances for the influencers he heard were coming to town. One more thing to add to his ever-growing list. Jake unlocked the door and walked in between the maze of stacked boxes waiting to be unpacked and put up on the shelves. He ignored them all and made his way to the counter near the register. He sat on the top of the step ladder and took a bite of the bagel. His stomach churned. He threw the rest of the bagel onto the counter.

Why had he bought the thing? He wasn't even hungry. He already ate pancakes.

He hadn't thought of Melissa in years, and now she'd entered his mind twice in one morning.

Jake spent the next few hours trying his hardest to forget this morning ever happened and started unpacking inventory boxes and following the schematic shelving plans his sister made for him.

His stomach growled. Pulling out his phone, he checked the time. Like clockwork, it was nearing lunch. Rather than going back to the cafe like he usually did, he reheated his unfinished bagel. While eating, he scanned the area and was impressed with the progress he made. Susan would be thrilled that her shop is finally coming together.

The light wood and glass shelving along the walls paired well with the light-colored walls. The store had a Scandinavian vibe, and together with all of the merchandise, it made it seem like each retail item was its own piece of art. Jake even found a box of evergreen garland and took the time to hang it from the counter near the register. He also hung a large wreath on the wall behind the counter surrounding her logo, SuSu's Petal Boutique, a play on her favorite holiday movie, *It's a Wonderful Life*.

He'd pick Susan up and bring her by later this afternoon to get her approval now that he created ample room for her scooter.

His phone buzzed in his pocket.

Susan's voice rang through from the other side. "Hey."

"Hey," Jake replied.

"I'm sorry for volunteering you. After thinking about it, I realize I overstepped my bounds. If I were in your shoes, I wouldn't appreciate someone offering me up for service either. I wanted you to know that I'll put a call in for Mayor

Jackson in a few minutes, but I wanted to apologize to you first."

Jake sat down on one of the few stacks of boxes left to unload. He sighed into the phone and rubbed his eyes with his thumb and forefinger, relieving the stress behind them. "Don't call her. I'll help. I mean, there are only a few days until the festival. Main Street's practically already decorated. They can't have much left to do."

"Jake, you're a doll. I'll call Andrea and tell her you're in. She will appreciate it."

"Yeah, yeah. I'm hanging up; got a lot to finish here if I'm to be the new assistant event planner."

He hung up the phone, shaking his head. "What did I just do?"

CHAPTER FIVE

"Jake Blessing," Melissa swallowed hard at the mention of his name. After all these years, he still made her heart thud like a jackhammer. She couldn't run into him. The last time she saw him in high school, she made a fool out of herself at prom. When she saw him and Molly dancing, her heart broke into pieces. Molly won. Then her teenage brain reacted poorly, confronting Jake the moment after she witnessed Molly kiss him.

She had been overwhelmed with her emotions that night, knowing he would be there with another girl. She had been too stubborn to tell him she liked him all year, and when she finally decided to go to the prom and tell him, it all fell apart. As an adult, she realized prom wasn't the place to tell him of her longterm crush, and her excuse for never wanting to talk to him again was pitiful. She accused him of being a jerk and taking credit for all her classwork. And being the stubborn girl she was, she gave him the cold shoulder the rest of the year.

When he returned to town the following year for Molly's graduation, she almost went up to him and apologized and begged for his forgiveness. She missed him terribly that year and regretted her behavior. But when she made her way toward him, and only a few people stood in her way, she stopped, staying back as he got down on one knee proposing to Molly. Melissa knew that it was truly over. A one-sided crush, her love never to be returned.

Melissa's mouth went dry, and she swallowed hard. She took a breath as her heart returned to a semi-normal pace. "What's he doing in town?"

Jenna, completely oblivious to Melissa's near-meltdown, got all bubbly and was practically bouncing. "Obviously reminiscing about you. He asked me if you were in town when I bumped into him at Walter's."

Melissa's eyebrows shot up along with her heart. "He did? Wait. Why were you at Walter's this morning?"

"Duh, getting my usual coffee."

Dumbfounded, Melissa blurted out, "Why did you ask me to spend my dwindling funds to buy you one?"

"Girl, I drank that three hours ago. I needed more. Andrew kept me up all night. I need my eight hours of sleep to survive." Jenna pulled a five-dollar bill out of her back pocket and handed it to Melissa.

Melissa rolled her eyes, shoving the money into the pocket of her jeans.

"Right!" She drew the word out skeptically. "You texted me practically three hours ago while you were in Walter's, telling me to bring you coffee ASAP."

Jenna dared to look guilty. "Okay, you got me. I was hoping by the time you went, which I knew would be nearing lunch, Jake would be walking back over for lunch. Walter gave me the scoop, and Jake goes every day around the same time. I wanted y'all to meet accidentally."

Melissa's stomach sank, and she thanked her lucky stars they didn't meet. "Seriously, Jenna."

"Well, don't get your holly in a bunch. My plan failed."

Melissa rolled her eyes at Jenna's Christmas cheer.

Jenna stuck her tongue out, took a large sip of her coffee, and her words jetted out of her mouth, the caffeine kicking in.

"If I succeeded and y'all met up, you probably would have come in here frantic with worry dissecting every word you said, wondering if you gave Jake the wrong impression. Especially after the way you dumped him at prom."

"Dumped him?" Melissa asked, exasperated at Jenna's interference. "I never dated him. How could I have dumped him? Plus, we were partners in class. There was never anything between us besides a class relationship." Lying through her teeth, she continued, "I could handle seeing Jake Blessing again. Seriously, the way you're acting is as if we are still sixteen. I am twenty-six now, I've had boyfriends, and a long-term one that I still speak to, I might add."

"Still speak to?" Jenna's eyes grew wide. "Why am I the last to know this? Tell me everything. When was the last time you spoke to Paul?"

Melissa's shoulders stiffened then pulled back. She put a hand on her hip, and her blue eyes narrowed at Jenna. "That isn't the point. The point is I've matured. I can handle a little conversation with Jake without freezing up if I see him."

"Good to know." Jenna bit her cheeks, trying not to smile but graciously changed the topic. "So, what are you going to do about becoming an event planner again?"

Melissa's indignation over her relationship with Jake fizzled out, and her shoulders slumped in defeat. Snicker-doodle was back from exploring the shop, and Melissa bent down to pick her up. "I can't let my dad or Andrea down. Plus, the woman who worked for Andrea probably had almost everything completed. My dad surely was wrong when he said she didn't have anything done. Seriously, I'll probably have little to do—being that the wedding and light festival is only ten days away."

"If you say so," Jenna said as she took Snickerdoodle out of Melissa's arms and cuddled her. "She really is adorable. I can't believe you've never sent me pictures. If I had a dog this cute, your texts would explode daily."

Melissa laughed, "My phone is full of photos; I'll make sure to start sending them to you."

As Melissa and Jenna walked around town shopping for gifts for the influencers, they also talked to several of the shop owners on Main Street and Marshall Street to start to make some changes to their decorations and gave them a few ideas, hoping that they would be able to make some quick changes before the influencers arrived.

When they walked up to Dorsey's Market to pick up a few items to add to the gift basket of local goods she and Jenna decided on for the influencers, Mr. Dorsey stood near his fruit display outside, and Mr. Fournier, the bakery owner, stood beside him. They looked to be having a heated discussion.

"I wonder what that's all about?" Melissa asked as she neared.

Jenna rubbed her hands together, excited for some new gossip to spread. "I'm about to find out." She walked quicker, making her way toward the two men.

Mr. Dorsey noticed them first. He huffed at Mr. Fournier then proceeded to wipe his hands on his apron front. "Good afternoon, ladies, Melissa, perfect timing. Maybe you can settle something for Maurice and me, being that you are soon to be related to the mayor."

"If I can, sure."

"Maurice was telling me that his grandson who works for the city council told him the town is having some financial difficulties and that these infuwazits who are coming into town are going to help bring us business. Is this true?"

This was the first time Melissa had ever been brought into anything related to politics because of her relationship to her dad and the mayor. This was something that was sure to happen again in the future, and she really had to think of how to answer without giving too much information.

She turned to Jenna, who lifted her shoulders as if saying, "I don't know what to say."

"Well, girl, tell this old fool it's time we both retire and leave town because we will lose more money staying in a dying economy," Mr. Fournier said after her long hesitation.

"Oh no! Mr. Fournier, you can't do that. Our economy isn't dying quite yet." Melissa was searching for something to say to make these men not want to close their businesses. Their stores had been open for generations in Cypressville. She turned to Jeanna, pleading with her eyes for her to help her out.

Jenna chimed in, "Once I found out which influencers were coming to town, I found out they are top-notch at advertising. Each one has over a million followers and increased tourism to all the locations they focus on in their posts. Hundreds, even thousands of tourists, start flooding in within days of their first post, and the tourists then start posting about how they met or saw the famous influencer, which increases business more. I am super excited to get more flow in my shop because of this, hopefully. I even saw some people who follow the influencers love the small towns they visit and end up moving there. If that happened here, our economy would flourish."

Mr. Dorsey and Mr. Fournier both seemed interested in what Jenna was saying. Melissa could see the idea of increased customer flow had its appeal. She scanned their street and noticed hardly any decorations had been put up here yet, and the festival was days away. They had a lot of work that needed to be done, and she couldn't wait to talk to Andrea.

The two men started bantering back and forth again about how one would sell more than the other as if they competed for the potential new flow of customers. As they were arguing over who would make more sales, an idea popped into Melissa's mind.

She blurted out, "I have an idea." Everyone turned to her.

"You know the influencers really love Christmas, and I noticed no one down your street has decorated very much." "And?" Mr. Dorsey said.

"Well," Melissa continued, "if you really want to get some notoriety on the influencers' blogs and social media, which is free advertising for you, I personally think you need to bring your decorations to the next level. I mean, you need to make it moviequality good. Make the influencers want to come down this side street and shop here."

The wheels in her head kept turning. "Mr. Dorsey, what if you made large fruit displays that are Christmas themed, and Mr. Fournier, what if you make like a giant gingerbread man people can take pictures with? That kind of display will surely bring people down here."

Both men looked at her as if she were nuts.

"Of course, those are just ideas, but whatever you decide, the influencers will be here soon. The tree lighting is Satur-day, and that is only five days away. Y'all would have to get to work today and have it done before... I'd say Wednesday, to really make a difference. Think of it as a contest. Whoever has the best display makes the most money."

The two men turned to one another and laughed. Mr. Dorsey turned to Mr. Fournier and held his hand out. "Challenge accepted. May the best man win."

The men shook hands, and Mr. Fournier turned to Melissa and Jenna. "Ladies, always a pleasure, but I must run. I have a lot of planning to do to beat this old fool." He took off across the street to his bakery.

Mr. Dorsey also said his farewells as he rushed into his store and hollered out for his manager to meet him in the office for an emergency meeting.

"Well, that went better than expected," Jenna said. "I think you may have inadvertently started a new tradition for these guys. Battle of the Christmas decorations. I can't wait to see what they end up doing."

Melissa giggled. "I have no clue, but it works out for us because that is one less thing I will have to do to get downtown ready for the festival. If I am going to do this, which it pretty much seems like I am, we need to finish these gift baskets, and I need to finish talking to all the shop owners to help them get with one another and make this the most magical downtown ever to exist. We have to keep this place from going bankrupt because I don't want to lose iconic stores because of lack of sales."

"Same here. My livelihood depends on this, too," Jenna said seriously.

Melissa linked her arm with Jenna's. "I know it does. Let's not tell everyone it's me planning, and I will do my absolute best to keep you and everyone else in business by making the influencers fall head over heels in love with Cypressville."

CHAPTER SIX

The next day arrived, and Melissa made her way into town, groaning at the inflatables still on display in the traffic circle. She would have to remove those soon and figure something out fast to wow the influencers. She parked her car in the lot next to City Hall and turned to Snickerdoodle seat-belted in her car seat. "We better get used to this because we'll be spending all of our time in town surrounded by Christmas cheer until the festival begins and the wedding is over."

She unbuckled Snickerdoodle, kissed her, placed her in the puppy tote. As she walked into the newly remodeled City Hall, she thought about how she missed the building's Old World charm but had to admit the modern touches to the atrium were beautiful. She ignored the hustle and bustle and made her way to the back of the building toward the mayor's office. Her nerves were on edge as she mentally berated herself about falling into the trap of becoming an event planner once more.

Melissa arrived at the receptionist area, surprised to see

Cheryl, another of her high school friends she hadn't talked to in ages sitting behind the desk. "Hi Cheryl, I didn't know you were

Andrea's new assistant. Is she in her office?"

"Hey, Melissa, I started a few months ago. Mayor Jackson stepped out for a few minutes. You're welcome to wait in her office. She won't be very long."

"Thanks, but I think I'll wait in the atrium. I heard your mom wasn't entering the gingerbread competition this year? Is she all right?"

Cheryl rolled her eyes and groaned. "She's fine. I think she is using her arthritis as an excuse to get me involved this year. Her favorite hobby has always been acting like a drill sergeant, and I got suckered into taking her place."

"Girl, I get it. That's partially why I'm coming out of retirement to help Andrea."

Cheryl's eyes widened, and her mouth made a perfect little O. Melissa's stomach flipped over at her slip-up, and she started backtracking.

"I mean, I would help with their wedding regardless of whether I was coming out of retirement or not because I am so happy for my dad and Andrea, but it was just a shock on short notice."

Cheryl's momentary shock immediately transformed into what Melissa took as pity. Everyone in town knew what happened, and she had hoped they had forgotten all about it. She didn't want to dissect the moment any longer and was grateful the phone decided to ring.

Cheryl mouthed, "Her door is open."

"I'll be over there when Andrea gets back. Have her text me," Melissa pointed to the atrium, reminding her she was going to be waiting there.

Cheryl nodded.

Melissa walked back to the atrium. The area was beautifully designed, with a few reading chairs near the exterior wall full of windows and a set of french doors leading out to a small courtyard where a few cafe tables were set up. She sat down in one of the plush chairs and put her puppy tote bag on the floor. Snickerdoodle was sleeping. She gently stroked her head, then stood, leaving the sleeping dog, and returned to observe the bare-treed courtyard, surprised it hadn't been decorated with any Christmas lights yet.

"That's rather odd," she said to herself.

"What's rather odd?" A deep voice boomed directly behind her.

Startled, she spun around, her heart beating irregularly in her chest. Jake Blessing stood so close to her that when she stepped back, she lost her balance, falling backward into the windows. He quickly grabbed her by the waist, sending butterflies into her chest as he pulled her toward him.

Breathless, she whispered, "Jake."

"You okay?" He let her go once she was stable.

The heat in her cheeks flared to life, heart racing faster, making her breathless. She took a few deep breaths, embarrassed and disgusted with herself that being this close to Jake made her want to swoon. Who thought like that these days? His concern for her became evident in the little crinkle between his brows—a trait he still had.

"Yeah, just startled. I wasn't expecting anyone to be right behind me." Melissa's frustration at herself bloomed within seconds when the realization struck. Jenna was right. She wasn't ready to have a conversation with Jake without questioning everything. "What are you doing here?"

Jake took a step back. "I have a meeting with Mayor Jackson."

Melissa's eyes squinted, mouth pursed, no he couldn't be here for the same reason. What are the odds? He must be here for something else, permits or something for his sister's shop. Jenna said she was injured, so he must be helping her.

Before she could ask him, Snickerdoodle's little barks reached her ears. She brushed past Jake, picked up the puppy, gathered her belongings, and took off down the hall toward Andrea's office without another word.

She sat down in one of the plush seats facing Andrea's desk.

Melissa was surprised that the office was still practically the same as the previous mayor left it, painted deep gold with builtin shelves all dark stained wood. She would have thought that Andrea would have changed her office with all the changes to the town. The only things that appeared personalized were the smattering of plants around the office and photo frames placed here and there on the shelves of herself and Melissa's dad.

Melissa blew out a deep breath, hugged Snickerdoodle to her chest. "I should have just come into Andrea's office from the getgo like Cheryl recommended, huh girl? Then I wouldn't have to be so embarrassed about practically falling into Jake's arms from being so utterly nervous around him."

Snickerdoodle licked her finger, and Melissa took another deep breath. "You always make me feel better. How did I handle my stress before you arrived? I'll never know."

Melissa continued talking to Snickerdoodle. "You know, if I had come straight here, at least, even though I would have been shocked to see Jake, I probably would have handled myself with more dignity. Why did I not only act like a klutz, but also run away, once again? He must think I'm mental."

She brought Snickerdoodle up to her face. "I promise when he gets here, I will do my best to pretend the past didn't happen and try to talk to him as I would any coworker or friend. I can do this."

Snickerdoodle made a little bark, making Melissa smile as if her puppy understood her and was encouraging her along the way.

CHAPTER SEVEN

Jake couldn't believe Melissa still didn't want to talk to him. It had been ten years since he gradu-ated, and he struggled to believe that she could hang on to a high school grudge. But then again, she had been stubborn back then. Maybe it only got worse as she aged. He shook his head and muttered, "Some people never grow up."

The moment Jake sat in one of the chairs facing the entryway into the building, a woman with tawny brown skin, wearing a navy-blue pinstriped suit, rushed in. He jumped up.

"Mayor Jackson."

Andrea turned toward the sound. "Jake, great, you're here.

Walk with me."

Jake strode up to her, keeping pace with her easily.

"Melissa should be in my office, and we can get started with the meeting."

"Mayor—"

Andrea interrupted him, "Call me Andrea."

"Andrea, I ran into Melissa a few moments ago. She seemed completely unaware that I'd be helping her."

Andrea turned to Jake. "Melissa..." She stopped walking and paused as if searching for the right words, then took a deep breath. "I am fortunate she agreed to help last minute, but unfortunately, she is completely unaware of her minuscule staff." She gave Jake a hard-eyed stare. "Aka you."

"Seriously, out of this entire town, you can't find any other volunteers?"

"Everyone is busy with getting their own business ready for the influx of people we're counting on arriving for the festival. A few influencers have already started checking in at the bed and breakfast. I was just there to welcome them to our town. Come on. I'll fill you both in on what needs to be done."

They walked the rest of the way to the office silently. Christmas music filtered in through the building's sound system, and Andrea's heels clicked in a steady stride over the art deco tiled floors. When they arrived at the mayor's office, Jake glanced at Melissa standing in front of the wood door holding her dog in her arms as if she were a life preserver. Her bottom lip was caught between her teeth, her blue eyes were wide and shifting warily between Andrea and him.

He took a deep breath, and it was as if she noticed his dread of this meeting. She started petting the dog more, but she immediately stopped when the little puppy squirmed in her arms and started whimpering. She took a deep breath, and a mask of calm enveloped her. Jake was slightly impressed. He turned to the mayor, who either didn't notice or ignored Melissa's behavior entirely as she made her way behind her large wooden desk.

Melissa hissed, "What are you doing here?"

Jake plastered on a smile and spoke through his teeth. "I'm your help."

Her mouth opened and closed in rapid succession. She turned her head to the mayor, eyes glazed and her cheeks a lovely shade of crimson. Jake stood more erect, shoulders back in pride as he one-upped her and her snarky attitude from earlier.

Andrea sat regally behind her desk, her hair pulled up in a clean knot. Her sharp pinstriped pantsuit and crisp white collared shirt reminded Jake of the president. She placed her elbows on the top of the desk and clasped her hands. Her two pointer fingers were straight up and tapping on her red lips, assessing them.

Jake sat in the chair beside Melissa, and turned to face the mayor. A smirk tilted his lips at knowing Melissa was fuming beside him, wanting the last word. That was how it always was with them in the past. His mouth started to curve up at the corner when Andrea interrupted his thoughts, snapping both Melissa and his attention back to her.

"Melissa, I can't begin to thank you for helping me out at the last minute." Andrea continued in a professional tone. "I understand you left event planning, and I don't want you to feel trapped, even though I'm sure Frank bamboozled you into helping me." An endearing smile broke across Andrea's face, and her body slightly lost its tension when she mentioned Melissa's dad's name. Just as quickly, the smile faded, and she sat up straight, back to business. "Which I appreciate. I would like for you to consider this as our wedding gift rather than a job. With all of that said, I however have standards, and this town depends on the outcome of the festival. I am depending on both you and Jake to make this year a success. We need to impress these influencers."

Andrea pushed back from her seat and opened her desk drawer, pulling out a black datebook and a large binder. She placed them on top of the desk, opening the datebook first. "Any questions before we go into the details?"

Melissa pulled out her notebook. "I noticed hardly any storefronts were decorated and already started talking to local business owners downtown yesterday. I am hoping they will decorate their shops to help lessen our load. I also noticed the atrium wasn't decorated. I'm assuming that we will need to get that ready also?"

Andrea nodded.

Before Melissa could ask another question, Jake asked, "Are we expected to be your wedding planner as well or just the festival?"

Andrea steepled her fingers again, resting her chin on them. "Of course, I hoped Melissa would finish the arrangements for us. I am overloaded with my obligations surrounding the Christmas events and a few time-sensitive financial decisions for the town. Elise left her binder with all of our notes—"

Her gaze turned to Jake. "I will be giving that to Melissa, who will designate what you will need to do."

Jake turned to Melissa, who looked like she swallowed a lemon whole. He wanted to laugh that working with him seemed to fluster her. He tuned the mayor out, sure he'd get a list of todo's from Melissa when the time came. Back in high school, she was always making a list in her notebook. She was an organizer, and that year she had helped him organize everything he needed to get into college. She had been a lifesaver until prom.

After ten years, he was still confused about what happened that night. He was surprised to see her there. The day he was brave enough to ask her to prom, she beat him to it by lamenting all the reasons she hated prom and wouldn't go. So, when Molly, another junior, asked him to prom, he figured he'd accept.

Molly was sweet and geeky like him. She loved anime, literature, studying, and anything having to do with the outdoors. Actually, she and Melissa were a lot alike. He couldn't wait for them to become friends so they could all hang out until the end of the year. He knew he was moving away for college and hadn't planned on falling for Molly.

He was glad to be graduating and finally moving away to start a new life; the only part he knew he would miss was Melissa, even though Molly had kissed him in front of the entire senior class, that was initially just an ego boost.

When he turned and saw Melissa coming his way, he probably had a sappy smile on his face. He waved to her and couldn't wait to tell her what just happened, but he never got the chance. She slapped him across his face in front of everyone, including Molly, then said to him that she never wanted to be his friend again because he stole her grade or something. He couldn't remember the details anymore, but he remembered the sting of the truth in her words. She never spoke to him again and ignored him completely, and when they needed to talk or work together, she became flustered and uncomfortable. He turned to Molly for consolation, and their friendship eventually grew and lasted even when he moved away for college.

Jake glanced at Melissa taking notes. He could see her making little boxes next to things. She still made a list. He laughed, and they both turned to him. He put his hand up and faked a cough.

"Excuse me," he muttered, and they started talking again.

He started thinking of all the ways he could foil their plans and embarrass her as she did him all those years ago, then he shook that thought away. He would not resort back to high school behavior. That was cruel especially since her career was destroyed last year by someone doing just that.

He'd be a grownup about all this; they were adults now. There was no way she could still be mad at him.

Jake watched Melissa for a few minutes, taking notes and adding things to her list. She had the notebook balanced on one knee and a calendar on the armrest. Her dog was incredibly well behaved, lying at her feet sleeping. She gazed over at him. Her pen fumbled out of her fingers, landing on the dog's head; it yipped, and her notebook fell off her knee, going in the opposite direction as she picked up the dog to examine it. All seemed well because instead of placing the dog on the floor, she put it in the tote. Melissa glanced at Jake again, and her cheeks turned scarlet.

The mayor had stopped talking while Melissa picked everything up. She waited patiently as if this was a natural occurrence.

When Melissa was refocused, the mayor continued and Jake tuned back in.

"I want my wedding to be magical." She brought the binder to Melissa. "These are the notes that Elise and I already put together. I trust you."

Jake noticed that all the steam deflated out of Melissa as she hugged the binder to her chest like a child. She looked up at Andrea.

"I want your wedding to be beautiful also."

Andrea bent down and gave Melissa a brief hug, and Jake heard her voice quiver as she whispered.

"I am so glad you feel that way."

When Andrea turned to walk to her desk, he noticed Melissa wipe a tear from her eye.

Melissa glanced at Jake and scowled, her cheeks flamed red again. Obviously embarrassed, he caught her. She took a deep breath, opened and closed her mouth, glanced at him again, took another deep breath, and lifted her shoulders, holding them back. Her entire body lifted as if she gained an inch in height. Her voice was strong and clear.

"I certainly hope you didn't think I didn't care. I know I've been rather curt at times since finding out about the wedding through Jenna and Walter instead of Dad and at times a complete recluse, but I am very happy you and my dad are getting married, and I only want the best for you both."

She glanced at Jake once more. He lifted one eyebrow at her in question, wondering what all was really going on. She shook her head. He didn't want to be interested, but now that he thought about it, this must be incredibly hard for Melissa. She had been close to her mom. Susan had told him that only six months after her mom passed, her dad helped head up the campaign for Andrea, and they hit it off. Six months later, they were engaged and planning a New Year's wedding. Only recently, they surprised Melissa by shifting the date to the weekend before Christmas. Susan believed it was to make new holiday memories, but he thought maybe it had something to do with the festival and the influencers after the meeting.

He stayed silent.

Andrea kept eye contact with Melissa. "Thank you." Andrea then walked back behind her desk and sat down.

It felt like a few minutes passed, and Jake assumed the meeting was over now that Andrea gave Melissa the book. He was about to ask if he was dismissed, but Andrea beat him to it.

"We have a lot to discuss."

It wasn't over. He slumped back in his chair and crossed his leg, resting his ankle over his knee.

"This entire debacle has increased my stress level. When Elise left to elope, I imagined the board of directors were meeting, ready to have a petition signed to remove me from office."

Jake interrupted, finally trying to get back into the conversation. "They wouldn't dare. Look at all the amazing changes you've made bringing this small town back to life."

"I appreciate your kind words Jake, but business is business, and sadly the town's financial situation is worse for wear because of my renovation project. We need to bring money back into Cypressville, and this festival is my last resort."

Andrea stood and started pacing with her hands behind her back. She stopped and stood by her window, looking out. Melissa fidgeted in the chair beside him. She looked like she was debating doing a runner. Then she sneakily shoved the binder in another tote bag. The mayor turned around, and Melissa sat up straight like she'd been caught doing something naughty. Jake wanted to laugh and once more covered it up with a fake cough. Melissa kept her eyes straight, but he saw her cheeks turn pink again. Having blond hair and ivory skin didn't help her. Poor Melissa had never been good at concealing her embarrassment.

When Jake turned back to Andrea, she was sitting at her desk again with her calendar once more in front of her.

"Now, let's get back on track." She tapped her pen point on the datebook. "I can't be in two places at once. That is why I had Elise planning everything. Now I'm depending on you both to make sure the festival runs smoothly. My wedding needs the most attention. Most of the festival events are planned. You need to follow through with getting things in order and organized. And as you can see, the majority of Main Street's decorations are completed, and the final touches should be all that's left."

She looked at her watch and stood. "I have another meeting to attend." She turned to Melissa. "Take your time packing up. I'll let Cheryl know to keep an eye out for when you leave."

Andrea was almost at the door when she turned back around.

"I almost forgot. Melissa, you and Jake have to represent my planning committee in the gingerbread contest. It's on the schedule for Friday, the evening before our wedding. It will be fun. Your dad and I entered it also this year."

She left the office, and Jake groaned. "You've gotta be kidding me."

The last time Melissa and he entered the contest, they ended up eating all their gingerbread and having an icing fight that got them disqualified.

They were both still sitting down, and when he turned to Melissa, they both laughed. The tension he'd been holding on to from the moment he sat in that office finally lifted.

Andrea popped back into the office. "Melissa."

Melissa jumped at her name, and they both turned to the door. Andrea looked at them warily.

"Are you both all right?"

Jake answered. "We're fine, just reminiscing on the last time we entered the gingerbread contest."

Melissa snorted and tried to cover it up, but when they all laughed, she did it again.

Andrea was the first to stop. "I came back in here to tell you, Elise and I were discussing having the reception in the atrium and courtyard. It's the only thing we never got around to planning, but I do have a caterer lined up. He is waiting on a call to tell him where he will need to deliver. I need you to call him today and let him know this is my final decision. His number should be in the binder."

Andrea didn't wait for a reply and turned to leave.

CHAPTER EIGHT

Jake walked beside Melissa as they left the office. She waved to Cheryl, who was on the phone, and shifted her tote bags over her shoulder.

"You took quite a few notes in there. Is that indicative of what needs to be done?"

Melissa stopped walking. When Jake realized, he stopped and turned around. Melissa was taking a deep breath. He watched her face go from anxious to determined. He wondered if she was like this with everyone or just him. He didn't remember her being so awkward around him in the past. Finally, she seemed to make some sort of decision, started walking again, and met up with him.

"Yes and no, it's a habit. I like to make notes while my clients speak about their ideas and plans, on the little nuances of their body posture changes or inflections in my client's tone."

"Interesting. So what little nuances did you gather from Mayor Jackson?"

Melissa stopped walking and turned to Jake. "Remember

when Andrea spoke of the influencers? Did you notice anything particular during that moment?"

Jake stuck his hands in his jean pockets and tilted his head up in thought for a moment. He didn't remember anything about influencers. That must have been when he was reminiscing.

"Nothing stands out." Jake lifted his right eyebrow in question. "What did you notice?"

Her mouth lifted in the corner into an almost smile, causing a dimple to appear on her left cheek. He used to love making her smile like that. As if they had an inside joke that only the two of them knew. He tensed when he realized where his mind was going. He folded his arms over his chest and tried to pay attention to reading her lips.

"Her body shifted in her seat. She uncrossed her legs, putting both feet flat on the floor. She sat more erect, but her hand picked up the corner of her planner and started flicking the edge with her fingernail, and lastly, her voice hitched and sped up."

Jake whistled softly. "Wow, all that."

He barely heard a word she said. He forgot how full her lips were, and with the pink tint on them, he wanted to kiss them. He shook his head, trying to get that thought out of his head. He didn't want to start anything with Melissa. She had issues, and she was drama. He didn't need that in his life.

"Yes, all that." Melissa rolled her eyes at him and started walking toward the atrium.

Jake didn't want to leave her yet, so he trailed behind her and asked the first question that popped into his head.

"What does that tell you about our client?

"Our client? This is not a job! You heard Andrea. I am helping my dad and my future stepmom." She exhaled and started walking faster as if she were trying to escape.

"Wait up! It was just a joke. Seriously, what did you discover? I'm curious," Jake asked as he caught up with her.

Melissa gripped the strap of Snickerdoodle's carrier hanging from her shoulder. Jake didn't like making her stressed out, but they had to work together. He needed to figure out some way to make her feel comfortable with him.

He could see she was trying to take a deep breath. Had she developed anxiety since high school? He didn't want to pry, but they would be working closely together for the rest of the week. She's going to have to get used to being near him again after so many years.

He wanted to give her space, so he still kept up with her hurried pace but not quite beside her. She stopped again without warning, and he nearly knocked her over, he grabbed her shoulders, and her bag swung, causing Snicker-doodle to whimper.

She gave Jake an evil eye and pulled Snickerdoodle out of the carrier, kissing her head, murmuring, "It's okay, the mean man didn't mean to hurt you." Snickerdoodle returned the kisses with little licks onto Melissa's chin.

Jake stood there watching her transform before his eyes, stressed out one minute glaring at him like he was a horrible monster to accidentally hurt her dog, then loving and calm the next while making sure her dog was alright. The dog had to be some kind of therapy animal.

The animal must have been, because Melissa turned to Jake in the next moment, surprising him. "Do you want to grab a coffee? I can explain what I discovered, plus we have a lot to do to help bring this festival to life and make my dad's wedding a magical event for Andrea."

Jake was utterly flabbergasted. He took his hand out of his pocket and ran it through the side of his hair, trying to hide his confused but relieved smile. He wasn't ready to stop being around her, no matter how nutty she seemed to be now. Something about Melissa had always drawn him in like a moth to a flame. And she was doing it again. He pretended to think over her offer.

"Sure, I guess."

His moment of victory back in Andrea's office was reversed. The ball was back in Melissa's court.

CHAPTER NINE

They walked into Main Street Java, and Walter was at the register. He eyed them walking in together, and a huge grin graced his lips. "Melissa and Jake together again! I haven't seen you two together since you were in high school. I for sure thought back in those days, you two would have been the ones getting married out of high school. Y'all were inseparable for a time."

Melissa's cheeks flushed, and Jake cleared his throat, both clearly uncomfortable. Jake spoke first, ignoring Walter's statement. "I'll have my usual." He turned to Melissa, whose cheeks were still scarlet. "What will you have, Lissy?" Her old nickname flew out of his mouth as if no time had passed.

She turned to him quickly, eyes startled, and she knew her blush spread to her neck and décolletage when Jake's eyes flickered down, and he gave her that same cocky grin from back in high school. He always would try and embarrass her by saying outrageous things to get her to blush "all the way down," as he used to call it. The last time he made her blush that hard, he asked her if she blushed below the belt. With that thought in her head, she bit her lip and stared at him, wondering if he remembered too.

Jake cleared his throat, turned back to Walter, cleared his throat again, and pulled out his wallet. His voice cracked on the first word. "My treat." He cleared his throat again. "Keep whatever we need coming, and I'll pay when we're done with our meeting if that's all right?"

"Sure, sure. See me after." Walter turned to her, and she stared at him mutely.

"Lissy?" Jake urged, "Walter needs your order."

Jake was the only one ever to call her Lissy. Hearing it on his lips melted her heart. She missed the way it flowed out of his mouth. Almost as if her name was sacred. The last time she heard that name was the night of prom. She had been jealous and upset with herself for being so mean to Jake. He had been hurt and confused and completely clueless that she was in love with him. The pained, confused look on his face when he called out her name pleadingly, to explain her actions as she strode away without turning back to apologize, was one of the hardest things she ever did in her whole life. Including last year's horrible planning event. She shook those memories away, finally answering Walter with her order.

"A mocha latte, a Puppuccino, and one of your ham and cheese croissants."

Turning to Jake, she focused on the collar of his jacket, not wanting to get lost in his eyes or focus on how his shoulders were broader and his jawline stronger. His beard shadow was even darker. Jake, the man, made her heart flutter ten times more than Jake, the teenager. Before her cheeks could turn red again, she said, "I'll go find a table."

The only open table was in the middle of the cafe. She placed her puppy tote on it and pulled Snickerdoodle out. This sweet little dog was one of the biggest blessings ever to enter her life. Snickerdoodle instantly calmed her nerves and gave her strength.

She put on her leash, and when she moved to take Snickerdoodle outside to the bathroom, she caught Walter's eye. She pointed to the dog, then outside. He nodded his understanding. Jake turned; her message obviously passed along.

Walter's comment and Jake's use of her nickname took her back in time to a place she wasn't sure she wanted to return. Jake made her nervous, he made her want to feel again, and that scared her. The loss of her mom was tragic, and she didn't want to lose anyone else. Melissa groaned, then whispered out loud to Snickerdoodle, "Poor Jake, I keep forgetting his wife died. That has to be just as hard or harder."

If she were married to Jake, and he died, she knew her world would end. With that thought, she knew she could never fall for him again. She had to stay strong. She wouldn't ever allow anyone to get close to her again; she already had too many people in her life that she worried about.

The fresh air and focusing on Snickerdoodle helped calm the fluttering of anxiety building in her chest. As she paced the patch of grass waiting for Snickerdoodle to do her business, a memory washed over her of when she used to dream of Jake being her husband and secretly writing "Melissa Blessing" all over her notebook.

She growled to herself, frustrated.

"Girl, get those thoughts out of your head." She turned to Snickerdoodle and told her, "I can't love him. He chose Molly. He never saw me as anything more than a friend. Plus, it's dangerous to get serious."

Snickerdoodle yipped in response.

"You're right! I can never forget he is only friend material. You are such a smart girl."

When she went back in, Jake was at the table, smiling and

wiggling the Puppuccino. "I didn't know dogs could drink coffee."

Tension released when Melissa laughed, a genuine laugh, at Jake's goofy expressions he was making all of a sudden.

"It's not coffee, just straight-up whipped cream."

"Ahh. That explains the pure joy on her face licking it then.

Who doesn't love whipped cream?"

"Right!"

After that, the initial tension in Jake seemed to ease also. Melissa wondered if he was as nervous around her as she was around him. Relief swept through her at that thought.

He placed his coffee mug onto the table and pushed his flannel shirt sleeves up to his forearms. He grabbed onto the handle of his mug, and the forefinger of his other hand rubbed the rim in circles. He seemed mesmerized by the motion; he then lifted his eyes to hers.

"So, tell me. I'm curious, what did you find in the mayor's mannerisms?"

Melissa wanted to melt. The intense heat he put off with those hooded eyes and leisurely posture was implying flirting. Was he doing this on purpose to play with her? He couldn't be flirting, could he? She took a deep breath, pushing that to the back corner of her mind. She had to be professional. She placed her coffee on the table and dove into one of her favorite things about her job.

Old job, she mentally berated herself.

She closed her eyes, visualizing the meeting with Andrea; when she looked up at Jake, his finger stopped circling the mug and both his hands dropped to his lap. She smiled. Maybe he was feeling some of their old chemistry after all. Her smile widened as she started to explain her process.

"Well, when our conversation with Andrea began, the first thing she did was sit straight, and her voice increased speed by a fraction, leading me to believe she was excited about the influencers coming. But as she started talking about their arrival and Elise not being here, she briefly gave me a sympathetic look, pulled out another planner, and started to flick the corner of a few pages. Those actions told me she was out of her element and nervous about what might happen."

"Very observant. I didn't notice any of that. To me, she was just sitting at her desk."

Melissa nodded. "Most people don't pay attention to the little shifts. At one point in time, I believed this gift was one reason I became successful in my past career, but even I stopped paying attention toward the end. I had too much on my mind, but that is neither here nor there." She took a sip of her latte and then said, "Andrea wasn't joking when she said how important the influencers' reviews and videos would be. I researched a few of the influencers in depth last night online. Yesterday, Jenna showed me a couple who were coming on social media, and let me tell you. They are no joke. People flock to wherever they go within days." She chuckled. "Boy, you should have seen some of these guys. They are over the top in love with Christmas. I see why Andrea was nervous yet appreciative about me taking this on. She knows Christmas isn't my thing."

"Your thing? You used to love Christmas, from my recollection. You and your mom would go all out for the holidays."

Without warning, Melissa's eyes started blurring. She blinked rapidly, trying to prevent tears from falling and embarrassing her in front of Jake. Thankfully, he tilted his head down, picked up his mug and watched his coffee swirl for a moment, and changed the topic.

"What do the over-the-top influencers being here mean for us? I thought almost everything was done?"

Melissa pulled herself together and put on an artificial smile. "It means we need to turn this town into the best Hallmark® movie set by the night of the wedding. That's what these people are after, an enchanted magical Christmas with a Hallmark® ending—hopefully, that will be Andrea and Dad's wedding." Melissa took the first bite of her croissant. Jake followed her actions and did the same with his.

Melissa continued their conversation. "Andrea had the right idea keeping the wedding a secret from the influencers. I looked through every single post and blog last night, and none of them ever witnessed a surprise wedding. We have a lot of work to do."

"Great." Jake slumped back in his chair and finished off his sandwich.

Melissa felt a bubble of happiness surge forward as Jake pouted. This Christmas might not be so horrible after all. For some reason seeing Jake uncomfortable made her feel giddy.

She brought Snickerdoodle to her nose, covering the enormous grin taking over her face, and whispered in her puppy's ear,

"Do you think I'm mean, being happy he's put out by this?"

She peeped over Snickerdoodle's little head. Jake grumbled to himself just like he used to when they were in school and she'd talked him into doing something he didn't want to do, like when she dared him to jump with her into the cold lake, which he did, but she stayed behind laughing. She was cruel, but the memories of them laughing and him being a good sport even though he pouted warmed her heart.

She bent over to place the dozing Yorkie in the carrier, forgetting her promise to herself not to fall for Jake again.

She whispered, "Don't tell anyone, but it feels good to be with him again." Snickerdoodle yawned, licked Melissa's finger, walked in a little circle in the carrier before settling and falling fast to sleep.

Melissa and Jake discussed plans for the festival, the wedding, and Jake's schedule for the next two hours. They decided to get started the next day on the events and activities and what type of gingerbread house they would make this time.

CHAPTER TEN

*W*ednesday morning, Melissa's dad walked in on her rummaging around the kitchen humming Christmas carols while starting the Keurig.

"Someone sounds like she's in a good mood."

Melissa walked around her dad and kissed him on the cheek.

"I am."

She happily returned to the coffee maker and pulled her cup out. She yawned while adding some peppermint mocha creamer. For the first time since her mom passed away, her heart felt light.

"Rough night?" her dad asked, pointing to her laptop, magazines, and vision boards spread throughout their island bar area.

Melissa yawned again and made a squealing noise while she stretched.

"This, dear Father, is all the plans for your wedding."

Her dad whistled. "That looks like a lot of work. I thought Elise had most of it done."

"I wish. I mean, I know that you only proposed a few

months ago, and the wedding was moved up only a couple weeks. Before that, planning for the festival was considered a priority, but I have a hard time believing Elise was waiting until the wedding week to plan anything. I called Andrea last night, and she couldn't find any other planners or notebooks of Elise's for the wedding. Andrea was panicked when the only thing in this binder were the dates and notes Andrea gave Elise the first day they sat down together."

"I need to call her." Frank rose suddenly, searching for his phone.

"Chill, Dad, I calmed her down. I told Andrea not to worry and that I would take care of it all."

Her dad's expression changed from worry over his bride to pity. "Sugarplum, I'm sorry you have to do this. I know it's not what you wanted to do, especially at this time of year." He stood by the table and picked up the nearest paper, held it up for her to see. It was the seating chart. "You did all this last night?"

"Yep, sure did."

"Wow! You are incredible. This is practically the whole town," he said as he scanned all the names listed near the tables on the charts. "What time did you wake up to start all this?"

"What do you mean wake up?" She laughed. "I haven't slept." "That must be it!" He slapped his hand on his leg and laughed. He walked around the island where Melissa was sitting at the attached bar and tousled the hair on the top of her head like a child.

"Stop it, Dad," she said as she shifted away from his horseplay. "What must be it?"

"Your good mood. It's only here because you've gotten slaphappy, honey. I haven't seen you like this in a long time."

"Ha! Ha! You think you're so funny." She grumbled and laid her head down on her arms resting on the island. "I'm so tired. I don't know how I am going to make it all day, but now I have a plan for your wedding."

"Thank you, Mel. I appreciate you doing all of this."

"No problem," she said drowsily.

Frank sat at the barstool next to Melissa, and his knee nudged hers. "So, what do you have planned for our wedding?"

"Not telling. It'll be a surprise." Melissa then started laughing and couldn't stop. She sat up, holding her stomach from laughing so hard.

"You okay?" her dad asked worriedly.

She couldn't stop laughing. Tears started falling, then she snorted. That was when her dad joined in. Frank's worry turned into side-splitting laughter. When she snorted again, she sat up, wiping away the tears with the hem of her sweater and taking deep, gasping breaths. Her laughter stopped, but a smile still graced her lips as she turned to face her dad. He, too, wiped his eyes, still smiling at her. She chuckled again.

"You're darn tootin right I am slap-happy! Gosh, this coffee isn't strong enough. If I'm going to be sane when going to my planning committee meeting, I need more sustenance than this." She took the last sip of her coffee as her dad started talking.

"I'm headed into town to meet Andrea this morning to give the influencers a tour of the town. Do you want a ride? I'm not sure I trust you driving drunk off sleep deprivation."

Melissa gave him a sharp stare, gathered all her papers, and placed them in a tote bag. When she turned to leave the kitchen, she nearly flipped over the barstool next to her and had to grab onto the island so as not to fall. Her dad tried to hide his chuckle, and she gave him another hard stare. He put his hands up like he was under arrest, then made the motion of zipping his lips.

Melissa tended to become incredibly clumsy when

exhausted. She sighed after her phone fumbled out of her hands like a dead fish. Her jovial mood seemed to disappear as the frustration of incompetence flooded her.

"I'll send Jake a text seeing if he can be the designated driver.

You're probably right about the driving." "Jake who?" Frank asked.

Melissa didn't look up from her phone. "Jake Blessing." After a few seconds, her phone dinged.

"That was fast—he said he could drive. Perfect! He wants to meet at Walter's in a few hours. Thank goodness for small favors. Once I get some shots of espresso into my veins and hopefully wake up, he won't notice how goofy I am, and we will be able to get the last of the festival things worked out. Are you all right with dropping me off there?" She looked up.

He gave her a brief nod over his coffee cup.

"Sure. You don't mind going into town early?" His eyes were gleaming with mischief.

"Nope, hopefully, I can get some more work done."

Melissa started humming "We Wish You A Merry Christmas." Frank got up and started handing her stacks of papers to put in her tote.

"Is this the same Jake that you were crushing on in high school?"

Melissa's head lifted from her task so fast, horror-struck that her dad remembered. Frank hurriedly turned around and picked up his coffee cup, trying to shield his smiling lips, but nothing could hide the twinkle in his eyes.

Melissa felt her entire face and neck heat up.

"Shut up, Dad."

She started moving around, grumbling. Sleep deprivation sucked. If only she'd been more alert, she could have prevented the teasing she knew was to come. Instead, she acted like a teenager and stormed out of the kitchen on the wind of her dad's chuckle.

How did he remember Jake after all these years? Of course, he had to have a perfect recall. He was the one to find her notebook with her and Jake's name scribbled all over the insides. It took months before her mom put a stop to his teasing.

Her dad shouted to her from the kitchen, the smile in his voice ringing loud and clear.

"I'll be leaving in ten minutes. You might want to freshen up a bit before we leave, maybe brush your teeth and use extra mouthwash." He finished with kissy sounds and a booming laugh.

CHAPTER ELEVEN

$\mathcal{A}$fter four espressos and a couple of hours sitting in
Walter's cafe, Melissa finally hoped she had
enough liquid energy inside of her to pass herself off as
awake. Her knee was bouncing. She jumped upright,
shouting Jake's name when he was standing right in front of
her all of a sudden. She knocked the table in her exuberance
and hurriedly held it with both hands, preventing everything
from spilling.

A few papers fluttered to the floor next to Snickerdoodle,
sleeping in her tote. Simultaneously, as they bent over to pick
up the papers, their heads knocked. They both uttered exple-
tives but still picked up the papers. Their hands grazed,
sending a zing of awareness through Melissa. Their eyes
connected and her heart started pounding in her ears.

"I didn't see you get here."

"I can tell."

His eyes crinkled in the corners, and her eyes moved
toward his full lips, spread wide, showcasing his perfectly
straight white teeth that practically gleamed like a television
ad.

Melissa blinked rapidly and thought, *Dear Lord, I need more sleep. I'm starting to hallucinate.*

Jake waved the papers in her face, breaking her continued stare. She felt like a fool and hurriedly sat in her chair. Her cheeks heated up profusely. He sat and placed the papers on the table, then tapped his finger on the top.

"Looks like you've been working here for a while."

Melissa started shoving the papers in her tote, trying to hide her nervousness around him. Not paying attention to what she was doing, the papers were all getting crumpled. Her only thought was about how good-looking he was this morning. He smelled like a blend of essential oils. Did men wear essential oils? She wanted to shove her face in his smooth, freshly shaved neck and inhale. She felt her eyes close and her body leaning in toward him. When he cleared his throat, it shook her out of her daze.

Her cheeks heated, and she hurriedly turned back to the table and folded her laptop. Jenna was so right. She would never be ready to face Jake. She thought she'd grown up and out of her awkward teenage self; by gosh, she was twenty-six years old and dated since her crush on him, but it felt like he affected her more now than he did back in high school.

This was all her dad's fault for embarrassing her this morning, reminding her of her unrequited first love. That had to be it because yesterday she had been cool around him, angry at first, but it worked out, and they had a great few hours sorting through what needed to be done.

"Well?" Jake said.

Melissa stared at him, eyes glazed over as if starstruck, and her tongue finally went into action—her brain not so much.

"Well, what?"

He sort of snorted but wore a half-grin, tilting his head slightly, his hooded eyes doing their sensual thing, making her heart thud harder in her chest. After a few seconds of no reply, Jake cocked his brow. Melissa huffed out a breath she didn't know she was holding. His hazel eyes were mesmerizing and sexy as heck.

Jake's full lips were moving again. Melissa finally forced herself to tune in.

"Have you been waiting here long? Scratch that. Do we need to reschedule? You seem a little out of sorts today?"

He stood up as if to leave, and his words finally broke the spell.

Melissa stood up too, stepping closer to him. "Gosh, I'm exhausted. I've been up all night organizing. I definitely don't want to reschedule. We have too much to do, plus I have a surprise for you."

He brought his hand to his chest in mock surprise, "For moi?"

"You're still a goof." She knocked her shoulder with his like olden times and grabbed his arm without thought, linking hers through his.

Jake stiffened slightly but didn't move.

"What's on the agenda?"

When Jake stiffened, she internally freaked out. It was an old habit to link arms. How could she forget she hadn't talked to him for ten years because of her foolishness? She unlinked her arm and bent down to pick up Snickerdoodle's tote and her other bag. "Do you remember the old Holstead Farm out on Highway 107?"

Jake took the other bag out of her hand and swung it over his shoulder. He looked adorable. Her hand fluttered to her chest, wishing she could take a picture. Here was a rugged man carrying her hot pink quilted tote that read "Princess" without seeming to care one whit what anyone thought. A genuinely endearing quality she didn't realize she liked in a man until that moment.

"Yeah, are they still in business? I thought Old Man Holstead passed away not long after I moved, and the family sold the property."

Grateful that she was paying attention to his words and not daydreaming anymore, she was able to keep a conversation going, finally. "One of the grandkids bought the farm from the rest of the family. It's still there."

"Okay? Is that where we are going?"

"Yep, do you need the address for GPS, or do you remember how to get there?"

"It's been a while, but I'm sure once I'm on the highway, I will remember."

Melissa hid her burgeoning smile behind her hand. "So, GPS it is."

"Ha! Very funny."

Jake opened her door for her. When she had climbed into the

SUV, he turned to her. "Well, what are you waiting for?"

Confused, Melissa asked, "What do you mean?"

He smiled, pointing to his GPS. "Plug it in. I'm not so macho to admit I depend on a map. I use them all the time in the city. They come in quite handy."

CHAPTER TWELVE

Melissa plugged in the address, and twenty minutes later they turned into the parking lot of Holstead Ice Arena. She took a wiggling Snickerdoodle off her lap and placed her in her tote. As Jake parked near the entrance, he said over the little yaps of the puppy. "I'll be. I would never have expected our area ever to get an ice-skating rink."

"I know, right!" Melissa replied. "George Holstead's granddaughter married a Canadian pro hockey player. After an injury forced her retirement, they moved back home and bought this place a year ago. Now they teach skating lessons, have free public skate nights, and even started a hockey league! Pretty cool, huh?"

Jake chuckled. "You sound like her autobiographer?" Melissa shot him a playful glare and then turned to stare out the window. Jake nudged her knee. "Alright, alright, seriously, this place is awesome for our little town. So, what made you want to come here?"

He must have thought he upset her. Melissa was more frustrated with herself rambling than upset with him. She turned her body in the seat facing him and tried to talk with a smile in her voice.

"I need to talk to them about putting up the outdoor ice rink that Elise ordered months ago. It was scheduled to be up by the end of the week, but I was hoping for this afternoon to give the influencers something more to do in town. Plus, I want to ask Sarah if they can put it up and decorate it to look like the ones in romantic holiday movies in under twenty-four hours. I really want to sell our town and to do that I need everyone's help ASAP.

Andrea gave me a list of vendors willing to donate lights and other Christmas decor."

"Good idea." Jake got out of the car.

Before Melissa had her stuff organized and was ready to get out, he was at her door, opening it for her. Her cheeks pinkened again, and he saw she had her bottom lip back in between her teeth. When she did that, it drove him mad. He had finally started to feel normal around her yesterday. Today, he practically kissed her inside the coffee shop. He had to get a grip on himself, but every time she got flustered, it drew him in. He wanted to fluster her more.

Her big blue eyes caught his, making his breath catch. They were full of emotions, as if she were searching his soul to see if he was trustworthy to be her friend again. Whatever he did in the past must have devastated her if she couldn't trust him. A section of her hair fell out of her bun. He swept it behind her ear. His thumb had a mind of its own when it brushed her soft rosy cheek lightly.

Melissa blinked; a radiant smile broke across her lips. The first he'd seen up close in ages. He'd forgotten that she didn't like smiling because her eye tooth was slightly crooked, but he loved that slight imperfection. It made her more beautiful.

Her thanks came out breathless and deep, and the brush

of her warm breath on his palm that still rested near her cheek made him pause and remember to breathe.

He took his hand away and shoved his now damp hands in his pockets, rocking on the balls of his feet for a few seconds, watching her exit the vehicle. He would not fall into the Melissa trap again.

He couldn't rekindle their friendship. It was starting exactly the same as it did in the past. Innocent touches that he interpreted as interest, but she only took as a dear caring friend. He couldn't bear falling into one-sided love again, and he feared that would only lead to her making up some lame reason to never speak to him again, and that was worse than not having a romantic relationship. He still missed her. He never stopped missing her.

He had to keep this strictly business.

Jake forced his mind to turn to Molly. Molly knew he loved Melissa; he never lied about that or kept it secret, but Molly was grateful for Melissa's abrupt end to their friendship. Jake probably never would have allowed himself to fall for Molly otherwise. He would have rather waited for Melissa to one day hopefully change her mind. In that respect, he was glad they stopped being friends.

Jake's circulating thoughts had him to the door quicker than Melissa. He waited for her. She was nearly at the door now. She was adorable, walking all wobbly on the gravel. He took a step forward to help, to give her a hand to hold. He stopped in his tracks—best not to have too much physical contact. She got closer, and he nearly burst out laughing. What had he missed on his way to the door? How had her hair gotten so messy from the car to here? Her bun was now a half-ponytail and no longer smooth. There were small clumps of hair pulled out of her bun near her scalp, almost in loops, as if her fingers were under them.

When their eyes met, the corners of her eyes were tilted

down, reflecting what he perceived as sadness. His heart dropped into his stomach, feeling horrible for the abrupt change in his mood. It wasn't her fault that he had unresolved feelings for her. He tried to shove those feelings back inside, but he couldn't wouldn't make her uncomfortable. They were only on the second day of working together, and he was determined to be the gentleman his parents raised him to be.

He opened the door for her. "I'm sorry, I was reminded of Molly for a moment and..." He let his words drift off because it was a half-truth.

He could see the moment his words filtered through to Melissa. Her eyes softened. The energy around them immediately felt like heartache. Melissa was new to grief. But he could see it in her eyes. She understood. It lurks up out of nowhere. But the grief he had today wasn't the loss of Molly. It was the loss of his and Melissa's easygoing friendship. He just used Molly as an excuse, which he felt slightly guilty for, and sent a silent prayer up to heaven asking Molly to forgive him.

She placed her hand on his forearm. The heat burned through his jacket.

"Jake. I'm so sorry, will you be okay? Do you want to leave? I can have my dad pick me up."

"No! No, I'm fine," Jake rushed out. Changing the topic, he said, "Is this my surprise, or is it later?"

Melissa blinked a couple of times, gave him another of those sad smiles, and thankfully got the hint. "It is. I thought while we were here, we could ice skate. Do you know how?"

He turned his head to the rink, "I've never ice skated before, but I used to rollerblade. Are they similar at all?" He looked hopeful.

She winked at him and moseyed past him, wiggling her behind.

"To me, they are different, but I'll let you be the judge of that. I'll see if Alex will give you a lesson."

He growled inside his head. She had to know what she was doing to him. Melissa took the tote off her shoulder, but as she was pulling it down, it snagged the low scoop neck of her sweater, practically baring her shoulder and the top of her... he wouldn't even look, but a vast amount of jealousy filled his gut when a man appeared in front of her, helping her get the bag unsnagged.

Grateful for her preoccupation, she didn't notice Jake's brief moment of insanity that filtered into him when she said another man's name. He shoved his hands into his pockets to prevent them from balling up and needlessly walking over to punch, who he assumed was Alex, in the face.

Jake moved toward her until he was standing inches away. Her body heat radiated through his clothes. He gave Alex a death glare from over her shoulder, and Alex took a step back and leaned against the counter with a snarky grin smattered across his lips.

"Thanks, Alex. Alex, this is Jake, Jake, this is Alex. Sarah Holstead's husband, the hockey player I told you about."

A flood of relief swept through Jake. Alex nodded congenially with a grin of mischief. He had a feeling they would end up being friends if he lived in Cypressville.

"Right. You didn't mention his name earlier."

He stepped around Melissa with his hand held out to Alex.

As they shook hands, Jake said, "Melissa mentioned lessons.

I've only rollerbladed. Are they similar?" Alex stood up. "What size shoe are you?"

"Twelve."

Alex hollered over his shoulder, his slight Canadian accent coming through, "Sarah, can you pull our new friend

Jake here some size twelve skates?" Then turned to Jake. "A lesson might not be a bad idea."

Melissa pulled her dog out of the tote and handed her to Sarah after she gave them all skates. Melissa put on a pair of figure skates then turned to Jake.

"I'm going to head out on the ice. See you in a bit." Jake put on his skates and stood, trying to find his balance.

Alex squatted down in front of his feet. "Let's make sure you lace them up properly." Jake felt like a kid when Alex relaced them.

"They have to be tight to give you proper support, or your ankles will wobble out on the ice." He stood up. We can't have you looking like a 'princess' for your girl, can we?" He slapped Jake on the shoulder, who still wore the hot pink tote bag.

Jake laughed.

He walked to the half wall surrounding the ice rink, watching Melissa. Alex came up beside him after he put his own blades on.

"She's gotten really good."

"She's amazing. She was such a klutz when we were in school.

I didn't expect her to be so graceful."

Alex turned to Jake. "Oh, so you two had a history?"

"We were best friends, then one day we weren't. Ready to teach?"

Jake quickly diffused any more personal questions. Even though he liked Alex, he wasn't ready to confide.

After learning the basics, Jake caught on fairly quickly. Melissa was right. It was different from rollerblading, but he had decent balance and picked it up quickly.

"Look at you!" Melissa shouted as he skated across the ice toward her. "You've gotten the hang of it." "I believe..." he started.

Then his hands spun out in circles trying to keep his balance. Melissa skated quickly to him, placing her hands on his waist, steadying him. Their eyes met, boring into one another's for a few moments. Jake brought his hands down, resting them on her forearms. The moment was broken when she lifted her hands off his waist, but Jake didn't let go. He slid his hands down her forearms to her hands and held them.

He couldn't help himself. He had to touch her. Screw the past. Today was the future.

She interlaced her fingers with his and started skating backward, pulling him along. Her graceful movements were easy to follow. On the ice, they didn't speak, just glided and enjoyed the moment.

After a few times around the rink holding both his hands, she let go of one, and he felt the loss of her warmth. She lifted the hand that was still linked to hers and spun underneath as if they had been dancing. Then, they were skating side by side, holding hands. They skated like that for another two laps to the sound of "The Christmas Song" playing over the speakers and the scraping of ice as their blades moved forward.

Holding her hand felt right. Jake turned to look at Melissa. Her cheeks were pink, not from embarrassment but from the cold and exercise. Her hair was still a mess; her eyes were happy. She was the most beautiful woman he had ever seen. He squeezed her hand, "You are amazing."

Melissa slightly tripped over her skate for the first time. He realized his blunder. He breathed out hurriedly, "I had no idea you could skate so well."

"Ha! Ha!"

"No, Lissy, I'm serious. You are so graceful."

She gave him an assessing look; obviously his expression satisfied her.

"I was horribly clumsy when I first learned. What you see today is after a year of lessons twice a week. I was in a pretty bad place the first time I came here. With the horror of my career maligned in print and still getting over my mom's passing, ice skating became my refuge. Sarah and I have become great friends since."

That was the first real conversation both Jake and Melissa had, and she revealed something incredibly personal. He wanted to say something but couldn't think fast enough. Melissa let go of his hand.

"Speaking of Sarah," she said. "I hear Snickerdoodle yapping. I think our playtime is over and it's time to discuss the ice rink downtown."

And professional Melissa was back. Probably for the best.

Sarah had mugs of hot chocolate in her raised hands. Snickerdoodle with a new sweater on and little boots was happily running around the tables. He smiled when he saw how happy it made Melissa.

When he got to the iron tables with built-in benches, he sat across from Alex and Sarah, beside Melissa, and whispered in her ear.

"Lissy, thank you for today. I needed this. Let's do it again sometime?"

"Absolutely." She breathed out with a radiant smile.

Yesterday at the ice rink was the breakthrough Jake and Melissa needed to rekindle their friendship. Last night they stayed out until after three in the morning when the town was asleep to make sure the surprise light show would work for the arrival of the bride when she traveled down Main Street. Melissa still wouldn't tell him what she had planned for the actual wedding march but kept hinting that it would hopefully make the influencers all swoon.

Jake arrived at breakfast late, whistling "We Wish You a Merry Christmas." Susan and Megan were almost done eating.

Megan turned to him with a mouth full of food and scowled. "You're late!"

"Megan, honey, we don't talk with our mouths full," her mom reprimanded.

Megan swallowed hard then observed Jake, who stopped whistling and seemed amused by her scowling face.

"Uncle Jake, why are you so happy this morning?" she asked, somewhat grumpily.

He passed behind her chair and tugged her pigtail braid. "What do you mean? I'm always happy."

Megan jerked her head away from another tug. "Uh-uh."

Jake sat next to her, and she turned to him and placed her little forefinger on his scowl line. "This is always scrunched up. But today, it isn't, and you keep whistling. Momma only does that when something really good is happening, like the time she got some extra money in the mail for her birthday."

Jake looked at Susan, who stammered, "Well, it is always nice to get unexpected cash sometimes, but Megan is right. You do seem extra cheery this morning. Did you have a good day yesterday with Melissa?" Susan's eyebrows were wiggling up and down, trying to be funny. "I mean you must have had a great night, being you didn't stroll in until dawn."

Before Jake could say anything, Megan crossed her arms over her chest and pouted.

"No fair, I want to meet Melissa. Momma told me y'all went to cut down a Christmas tree and went ice skating. I love ice skating."

Jake tugged her braid again.

"If I would have known, I certainly would have taken you. How about you and I go when I'm done helping out for the festival and before I go back home?" He turned to Susan. "And I guess you can come along too."

"Gee, thanks for the welcoming invite." They all shared a laugh.

Megan turned to Jake, "I don't want you to go home, I want you to live here forever."

He hugged her. "You never know, Megs, your wish might just come true." He kissed her on the head. "Now go get your backpack. You don't want to be late for school."

Susan hurriedly lifted her coffee to her lips, trying to hide her widening grin spreading at Jake as he hurriedly ate his toast. "So… how was yesterday?"

He glanced up at Susan, knowing she wanted gossip. He wasn't a gossip, and knowing she'd call Jenna and find out everything anyway he gave her a very bland and boring review.

"We got a lot done."

Megan came back in and was hovering near him. He ignored Susan's pointed stare at his evasive answer.

"You know what, the outdoor ice rink downtown is open. How about I pick you up after school and I introduce you to Melissa. What do you say?"

Megan nodded and started dancing around in circles chanting. "I'm going to meet Melissa."

Jake took the last bite of toast and was relieved Susan didn't dig more about his date with Melissa. It wasn't a date. He even had to remind himself it was just another outing— an outing designed for planning the festival. But somehow, when he revisited all of the time they spent together they always categorized in his mind as dates.

The conversation as they went out the door thankfully changed to the day's plans at the shop and what Jake needed to finish before the grand opening Friday. Susan would be returning to the shop with full force, and Jake would be free to spend every waking moment with Melissa finishing the last minute arrangements for the tree lighting and wedding.

Ten o'clock arrived and anticipation arose in Jake knowing any minute Melissa would be arriving. He didn't have to wait any longer as the bell on the door chimed and Melissa strode in with Snickerdoodle on her leash.

"Morning," she chanted.

"Morning." He just finished hanging the mistletoe tree near

the door. Susan had a wire tree made to display her handmade mistletoe balls. He turned to Melissa and Snickerdoodle. "Now that we have been getting to know one another again, I have a personal question."

"Uh oh, do I need to be worried?"

"Nah, it's really more of a curiosity."

Melissa picked up one of the mistletoe balls then glanced over the door. She almost looked disappointed.

"Well, what's your question?"

"Oh, yeah. Do you take your dog everywhere you go?"

Melissa picked Snickerdoodle up. "She's just a puppy and I read Yorkies shouldn't be left alone for more than a few hours or they can become anxious." She turned to the puppy. "We don't want that, do we? No, we don't."

The puppy wagged her tail excitedly as Melissa spoke to it. Melissa turned to Jake, who had been watching her baby-talk.

For some insane reason, hearing her baby-talk to the dog brought up visions of her holding his child in her arms. He had to be losing his mind. Who in their right mind confused a dog with a child? But this was the first time he allowed himself to dream of a family again. He thought that chance died with Molly. Not once since her death had he ever envisioned anyone but her holding an imaginary child until this moment. For the first time in years, the heavy weight of loss lifted, and real dreams for the future began to stir once more.

Jake backpedaled his thoughts when he noticed Melissa's cheeks were flushed. He averted his eyes to the right over her shoulder until the flutter of her scarf next to the delicate pale skin of her neck caught his notice. It moved in sync with what he assumed was her pulse. The idea of her pulse hammering away for him brought him into another wave of fantasy, one of desire where he moved the scarf aside and pressed his lips to the soft spot on her neck and felt the beats upon his lips.

He had to get his thoughts back on track, today was not about his one-sided attraction to Lissy; it was about business. He quickly brought his attention back to her dog. That topic was safe.

"Don't get me wrong, I love dogs, I was just curious why she was always with you. I don't mind her being with us, I like dogs."

She laughed, "You said that already."

He turned around to a box he had begun unpacking earlier before he started stalking the front window, waiting for her. He felt like a complete idiot and returned to stacking photo frames onto the shelf and tried another topic.

"It's day three of our partnership and only two days to go until the tree lighting and the wedding. What's on our agenda today?"

Partnership, what was he thinking? This morning was turning out so wrong. Susan was right; he obviously needed to start dating again if he was starting to create fantasies about a girl who had practically despised him for the last ten years. He needed to stop using work as an excuse and move on.

The heat in the room must have picked up—or his embarrassment, more likely. He pulled his sweater over his head and then pulled down his t-shirt that rose up with it. He squatted down to start unloading the box of picture frames.

He could hear Molly in his head the last time they spoke. It was the day he finally fessed up and told her he wanted to change majors from accounting to English and had been sulking around for weeks. He walked her to the car, and after she got in, she rolled down the window and called Jake back to her. "What are you doing to yourself, you big goof? Stop messing around and go after what you want. Dreams only happen if you make them. Mine sure did, and I will always support yours." Then she pulled him in for a kiss.

He didn't know that would be the last time he saw her. The accident took her life only two blocks from their apartment.

It was almost like Molly was with him again. He could hear her in his head telling him she approved of Melissa and was telling him once more to stop being a goof and go after his dreams. Molly was right that day. Even though it was a hard and depressing year, he was happy in his career.

Thinking of Molly didn't hurt or make him feel guilty for the first time since she died. Smiling to himself and feeling confident and cooled down, he turned back to Melissa.

She seemed frozen in the same spot, her eyes wide and slightly glossy, probably confused and wondering why he was practically drooling one minute then completely ignoring her the next. He was about to try and make some explanation up when she nearly sent him running for the woods.

Melissa sucked her bottom lip in then released it, catching it between her teeth. She couldn't have a clue at how incredibly desirable she was in that moment, holding that little puppy. He forgot he was holding a frame in his hand until it slipped out but thankfully caught it before it crashed to the floor, breaking the spell she had put over him.

He placed the frame on the shelf and said the first thing that he could think of to redirect his train of thought. "I told Megan today that I would take her ice skating at the outdoor rink and was hoping you'd come along."

"I wish I could, and you won't be able to either. We have to go out of town today and won't be back until evening."

Jake pulled his phone out of his pocket. "I'm going to text

Susan so she can call the school and let them know to put Megan on the bus."

"I'm sorry I've been so secretive about what we're doing each day. It's been fun to see everyone including you surprised at all the little changes."

Jake finished his text and returned his phone to his pocket.

"I don't mind. It has been fun and the town is really coming together. I overheard some of the influencers talking today at Walter's that they feel like they are smack dab in one of their favorite movies in the making. The effect you were aiming for is working."

"Woohoo! That is good news. Did you tell Andrea that little nugget of awesome?"

"Not yet, but I will." He leaned on the wooden shelves.

Melissa untucked her free-flowing hair from behind her ear, hiding her face from his sight. She held Snickerdoodle in one hand and turned to a shelf, reorganizing the candles with the other hand.

"Main Street Java is hosting this year's gingerbread contest." They both snickered. "We have to be on our best behavior this year."

"We will have a trusty sidekick to keep us in order. Megan will be our referee."

"Oh, that is so sweet." She turned to face him, her eyes all dewy, and gushed, "I'm looking forward to meeting her, and that will be such a fun activity for a kid. We will have to make something extra special and make sure we win."

"We sure will. So, today we are working on setting up the contest? That's tomorrow night, right?"

"Yes and that's the reason I want to work on this today. I want to get the influencers involved in the contest this year. I asked Bonnie Simpson to be the event photographer and have her also working on a selfie wall to hang up. I need to go over the final details with Walter, and after that, you and I are going to check out a sleigh."

Jake put the last frame on the shelf and compacted the box.

"What do we need a sleigh for?"

"The wedding. Overnight an idea started brewing, but I need to make sure Mr. McFarlan has what I'm imagining. He's my last resort, and if he doesn't have what I'm looking for he may have other options. Plus, I thought it might be fun if we tested them out."

"Don't you need snow for a sleigh ride?"

"Not this kind, I hope," Melissa said jovially as she finished rearranging the candles. She peeked in an open box on the table behind her. It was full of individually wrapped blouses. One of the blouses was opened and she put Snickerdoodle on the ground and held the flowered print in front of her. "This place is going to be a hit in town. We needed a shop like this."

"Yeah, I hope Susan does well. This has been her dream since the divorce; she wasn't sure if it would ever happen. Mom and Dad and I all surprised her with the purchase of the store. She almost didn't want to accept but it was too late by that point, the deal was already done."

Melissa lowered the shirt and gazed at him, her voice turned melodic. "You all bought this for her?"

"Yes, she deserved it. Susan is an amazing mom and being here is close to Megan's school, so once I'm gone she can walk to pick her up and come back here. We created a workspace with a little desk in the break room for her to do her homework."

Jake wished he could read Melissa's mind. Her expression changed lighting-fast and her back was now turned to him. He couldn't figure out what he said or what made her shut down. He watched her quietly opening the rest of the shirts.

She almost appeared melancholy. Did this remind her of her mom? That used to happen to him a lot the first year when Molly passed away. He watched her from behind and noticed her take a deep breath.

Her voice, soft and low, broke the awkward silence. "We've been so busy transforming the town and getting into a groove that I never asked, what do you do for a living back in the city?"

Relieved that whatever he said hadn't prevented her from making conversation, he happily responded to the topic change. "I work in publishing. I've been an editor since I graduated from college."

She turned back around; once again the light was back in her eyes.

"No way! You used to be so good at editing my writing, I should have you edit my book. I did all of my own edits and sent queries and my manuscript off to so many literary agents but got rejected by all of them. One was nice enough to give me feedback, Gwendolyn Jones, have you heard of her?"

"Yes, as a matter of fact, she's an agent to many of our authors. The company I work at is Sanderson Publishing. My friend Ben opened it a few years ago; we are really small but up and coming. Gwendolyn and I work together a lot, actually. I edit almost all of her clients' work. She's fantastic, one of the best agents we have, and incredibly kind. If she took the time to respond to your work and give you advice it must be special."

Melissa dropped the shirt she was holding back into the box. Her entire face lit up like a Christmas tree, and she practically pranced to her phone and bounced on her toes a few times. "I can't believe you said that; I swear I think she said almost the same thing."

His heart leapt into his chest, remembering her doing the exact same thing back in high school every time she got an A.

Jake had a goofy grin plastered on his face while waiting for Melissa to search her phone. She started reading.

> MELISSA,
>
> THANK YOU FOR SHARING THE FIRST FEW CHAPTERS OF YOUR BOOK WITH ME. AS A FIRST-TIME WRITER, I UNDERSTAND HOW DIFFICULT IT IS TO ALLOW SOMEONE TO READ YOUR STORY AND THEN GET A LETTER IN THE MAIL WITH THE SIMPLE WORD DECLINED, REJECTED, OR WORSE, NO RESPONSE AT ALL. A TASK EVEN I, AT TIMES, ADMIT TO DOING. HOWEVER, YOUR QUERY INTERESTED ME, AND WHAT I READ SO FAR KEPT MY ATTENTION. SADLY, IT IS NOT ENOUGH FOR ME TO SIGN YOU, BUT ENOUGH TO GIVE YOU SOME ADVICE. THE PROBLEM I SEE IS THAT YOUR CHARACTER'S VOICE LACKS DEPTH AND EMOTION. I AM NOT INVESTED IN HER. IN MY OPINION, AND THIS IS MY OPINION ONLY IF YOU WORK ON DEVELOPING YOUR CHARACTER, YOU MIGHT HAVE SOMETHING SPECIAL HERE. ONCE YOU DO, SAVE MY EMAIL AND SEND ME THE FIRST CHAPTER AGAIN. IF I SEE ENOUGH CHANGE, I WILL CONSIDER READING YOUR FULL MANUSCRIPT IF YOU SHOULD CHOOSE. GOOD LUCK.
>
> SINCERELY,
>
> GWENDOLYN JONES.

Jake whistled.

"I know! I have been frantically studying character arcs

and reworking my main character as I learn to understand what she meant."

"If you'd like, I can review your manuscript and advise you. I'd love to see how your skills have developed since school. Your stories were always the best. Actually, I'll one-up it. How about you let me edit your book? For free. I've been thinking about working for myself outside the company. You can be my first client and give me a review as a trade. What do you say?"

"I say, heck yeah! Who am I to pass up free help? How do you want me to send the file? I will do it right now."

Jake laughed, excited to see Lissy so animated, "Any document file is fine."

"Perfect. Give me two seconds and I'll get it copied and pasted out of another program."

Snickerdoodle started whimpering and Melissa turned to Jake. "Would you mind taking her out to potty? I don't want her to have an accident on the floor, and I have to send this to you now before I forget." Without looking up from her phone she said, "I left her leash by my purse."

When Jake didn't move, she glanced up at him and shifted her eyes to her bag and went back to her phone.

Jake walked over to the whimpering Snickerdoodle, picked her up, and walked to the leash. He was shocked at how tiny and light the puppy was and said to her, "You can't weigh more than a pound. We need to get some weight on you, maybe buy you a cookie from Walter." He clicked the leash into place and muttered, "I can't believe I was just talking to a dog."

CHAPTER FOURTEEN

Jake's phone pinged, receiving her email as Melissa exited the shop behind him, but he didn't pull it out.

He was completely focused on Snickerdoodle,making Melissa smile. Snickerdoodle was almost hidden in the grass that really needed cutting. She made a mental note to contact the city maintenance to have the grass cut today. They can't have anything distracting the influencers and everything needs to be picture-perfect.

In fact, she pulled out her phone and texted Andrea. Once she called the crew, Melissa had no doubt they would be out here within the hour. Andrea was a no-nonsense kind of woman, a quality Melissa admired.

She returned her phone to her pocket and her heart melted when Jake squatted down next to Snickerdoodle, petting her. She was practically the same size as his hand, and he quietly spoke to her.

Trying not to attract his attention, Melissa tiptoed closer and strained to listen to his whispered words.

"Come on, baby, do your business. Mommy's waiting for us inside, let's show her what a big girl you are."

Melissa covered her mouth with her hand to stifle her laughter. He was too cute and when Snickerdoodle tilted her head to the left to look at him, her little tongue slightly popped out, and he groaned, petting her head gently.

"You're melting my heart, sugar, but you need to be a big girl."

Melissa could barely contain her laughter. He was treating Snickerdoodle probably how he treated a real baby. It was so flipping adorable she wished she'd caught it on video.

Jake tried to encourage her to walk a little and Snicker-doodle rolled on her back, asking for a belly rub. Melissa couldn't take the cuteness anymore and snuck several pictures of Jake being suckered by the puppy. He obliged Snickerdoodle for a few seconds then picked her up, placing her on all fours. "I've got it! If you're good, I'll buy you a new sweater, one not so pink. How about something in plaid? Your mom used to love wearing plaid at Christmas. Maybe I can buy you girls matching shirts."

Snickerdoodle barked in agreement and immediately started to potty.

Jake stood up, laughing, "Typical woman, holding out for the bribe."

"Hey, I heard that!" Melissa half-shouted from behind him.

Startled, Jake yanked the leash a little hard, forcing a squeaky yap out of the puppy. As both of them rushed to soothe Snickerdoodle, they bonked heads. Before Melissa could think, Jake had her face in his hands and his lips pressed to her forehead, kissing where his head knocked hers. Her breathing picked up as she froze in place. His lips were warm and perfect and everything she ever imagined. She tilted her face up, pleading with her eyes for him to make the first move, to give her a sign he wanted to kiss her for real.

Jake's hands never moved. His breath held a hint of peppermint and coffee that lingered as he spoke in a soft deep tone. "I'm... Uh... Sorry, total habit, it's what I do when Megan gets a boo-boo. I wasn't thinking."

Her shoulders slumped as her heart sank into the pit of her stomach. So much for hopes and dreams. She got her sign. He wasn't into her. She was like his niece.

"What are you two doing?"

Melissa jolted out of Jake's hands, embarrassed at Susan's voice, hoping she wouldn't misinterpret the situation. But the massive grin she wore confirmed Melissa fears. Susan misunderstood.

"We knocked heads trying to save Snickerdoodle." Melissa tried to explain but it came out sounding lame.

Susan turned her knee scooter toward her shop.

"Right! Whatever you say. Don't let me interrupt. Y'all can go back to kissing boo-boo's." She laughed as she made her way in.

Jake shoved his hands in his pockets and stood there looking guilty.

Melissa glared at Jake.

"Thanks for trying to explain to her that isn't what happened."

She fumed when he didn't say anything.

"Jake, don't just stand there, go and explain to her it wasn't some declaration of love."

Jake rocked back and forth on his heels for a moment watching his sister scoot inside the store. He turned back to Melissa and tilted his head toward Susan, a huge grin on his face as if this were a non-issue. Her heart thrummed heavily in her chest to the beat of "Little Drummer Boy" playing over the town square. What if he wanted Susan to believe it? What if finally, after ten years, he was interested in her?

"Sorry about Sue, but if I go in trying to explain exactly what happened she will turn the whole thing into something absurd like me trying to cover up that we are secretly dating. If I keep quiet, she will eventually believe what you said as the truth." Melissa's brief moment of anticipation was dashed. Dejectedly she said, "She'd better."

She started to walk toward the door, all of a sudden exhausted and hating this job more and more because with every day that passed, she was falling more in love with Jake than ever. If anyone could see into her mind, they would think she was pitiful for falling in love with him a second time, and this time even faster. It only took a few days, not even the whole week.

"I need to get my things; we have a lot to do," she said and left him standing, holding Snickerdoodle's leash.

Jake pulled onto a gravel road. "Where to now?"

"Mr. McFarlan said to take a right at the fork in the road and it would lead to his new barn. That is where he wants us to meet him."

The fork appeared moments after Jake asked and he followed the directions. He bent down, looking under his sun visor at the monstrosity of a building. "That is no barn, it's a warehouse painted red with white x's on the door to look like a barn."

Melissa laughed then pointed. "There he is."

Mr. McFarlan, wearing his typical overalls and plaid shirt, stood beside a small door next to the biggest looking garage door she'd ever seen.

Jake exited the car and rushed over to help Melissa and Snickerdoodle out. She had the puppy already hooked to a leash and ready to go for a walk.

"Hello, you two. I have only two sleighs left, strangely they are popular all of a sudden. I even had two men haggle over the one I had for sale," Mr. McFarlan said as he held out his hand to Jake. "Long time no see, son. How have you been? Still riding?"

Jake shook his hand, "No sir, I haven't had time and they don't have any stables in the city."

"That's a pity, nothing like a good ride in the country to settle the soul."

Before Jake could respond, Mr. McFarlan hugged Melissa. "How's your dad, getting excited for his wedding?"

"Dad, excited? You know him, he doesn't show excitement, but I do know he is definitely ready to be married again."

"That is a truer statement than I ever heard. Now let's go look at these carriages. What are you needing them for, anyway?"

Jake was curious too. Melissa had been giving him a list of things to do when they aren't together, but when they are she likes to hold all her cards to her chest and surprise him as the days unfold. He didn't mind, and it was kind of fun seeing her do her event planning magic.

Melissa was the first to cross the threshold of the doorway when she stopped in front of them, clapping her hands together. "This is perfect, Abe!"

Mr. McFarlan walked in after her "Now tell me what you need it for and I can help you choose the best one."

Jake was impressed. This was not only a warehouse to store Abe's collection of carriages, but it was also a functioning barn connecting to horse stables toward the back. He used to love riding and helping out with the horses here when he was younger.

Melissa completely seemed to forget their existence and took off to examine each carriage. Jake smiled when Melissa did a little wiggly dance next to a Victorian-style carriage. As he watched her, he made small talk with Mr. McFarlan. "Abe, do you still let people come ride your horses?" "I do."

When Jake didn't respond right away Abe bumped his arm. "You going to finally ask that girl out? If I remember right, you were pining over her your entire last year of high school until you met Molly, Lord rest her soul, but I never thought that girl was quite as good for you as this one."

Jake turned to Abe. "Molly was the best wife in every way."

"I wasn't saying that, son, just that she wasn't the best one for you. That girl, she is your soul. I knew it back when you were a boy and I can see the way you look at her now. It's the same way, and I ain't never seen you look at your wife like that. Lord rest her soul."

Jake didn't know how to respond. Abe left him to his thoughts and went to talk to Melissa. They talked for a bit and started walking to a carriage that had a large covering over it. Melissa lifted up the edge high enough to look under it. She dropped the cloth and squealed in delight, doing a happy dance with Snickerdoodle that made Abe laugh.

His stomach fluttered. She was beautiful, her cheeks were rosy from the cool weather, her hair was a mess again from going under the cloth, and the happiness that exuded from her made his heart swell. Yes, he could admit he was attracted to Melissa, but was attraction enough to erase old memories? To start over? Being with her these past few days, there were moments where it felt as if time never stopped for them. He had a lot to think over.

Melissa made her way back to him. Abe held Snickerdoodle, following slowly behind her. She was practically skipping and the energy around her was electrifying. He couldn't help but smile as his heart raced from her nearness. She grabbed his forearms, sending tendrils of her excitement shooting up them. His hands wrapped around her forearms and before he knew it they were spinning around almost as if they were on the ice. Melissa's head leaned back with her laughter and when she stumbled he caught her.

She was breathless and smiling profusely. "Jake, I found exactly what I was imagining for Andrea. I can't wait to surprise her with it on Saturday."

Abe arrived with Snickerdoodle and handed her off to Melissa. "So, I will see you Saturday with bells on. Would you two like a cup of hot chocolate before you leave? The missus would love to see you both and would probably make me sleep in the barn for a week if I didn't bring her some visitors."

Jake and Melissa both agreed and followed Abe to his house.

The day went by fast. By the time Melissa and Jake finished their visit with Mr. and Mrs. McFarlan, they lost their opportunity to take a carriage ride and headed back into town. The roads into town were congested. The influencers were already making a difference.

"I can't believe a few hashtags on social media can bring in this type of traffic within a few days," Jake said as he tried to bypass some of the traffic by turning on Marshall Street instead of Main Street to get back to Melissa's car.

Sidewalk traffic was just as crowded. A crowd of people crossed the street while traffic was stopped and Melissa groaned. The bakery's enormous Christmas cupcake display practically blocked the sidewalk.

"What's wrong?" Jake asked as he slowed the car, stopping for pedestrian traffic.

"Christmas is what's wrong. Look at this." She motioned

with her hand to the bakery. "I know I suggested to some of the shop owners to decorate and make it like a movie set, but this is bordering on ridiculous."

Two giant, realistic gumdrops, wearing Santa hats and standing like sentinels, were in front of the entryway, and candy canes edged the walkway in front of The Old Tyme Candy Shoppe.

Jake laughed. "You're too focused on your side of the street. If you thought that was bad, you need to check out Dorsey's Market."

She sat up a little higher because the crowd of people that had crossed the street were now standing in front of the grocery store. Curious at what Mr. Dorsey decided to do to compete with Mr. Fournier, Melissa edged closer to Jake, trying to peer out his window. Without thought, she placed her hand on his thigh for support. The people slowly moved out of the way, and the few remaining were taking pictures, or they appeared to be using selfie sticks doing live feeds.

At the same time, they both said, "The influencers" and laughed together. When his breath brushed her face, Melissa felt heat rush up to her cheeks. She glanced down to his lips. When his thigh muscle flexed under her hand, she practically jumped back into her seat. She untucked her hair to hide her blush. She hated that her skin showed her every discomfort. If his leg hadn't twitched, she would have kissed him, then she would have really been embarrassed.

She bent down to the tote bag resting on the floor in front of her seat and took Snickerdoodle out. She tried to ignore her discomfort and pretend it was nothing.

Melissa brought the puppy to her lips, kissing her on the head and getting a little lick to the chin in reciprocation. She continued cuddling the puppy until the light turned green and placed her on her lap. Snickerdoodle circled around a few times and found her spot to settle.

With her nerves back in place, Melissa started to talk at the same time as Jake. They both chuckled. Melissa flung her hand out, about to say "You go" when Jake grabbed her hand. Her heart leaped into her throat, preventing the words from coming out. Jake interlocked their fingers and rested them on the console and gently squeezed her hand.

"You first."

Her mouth had gone dry, and she had to force herself to swallow. Two hard swallows and a single deep breath later, her heart finally slowed to a normal pace. The butterflies still bounced recklessly in her stomach but in a really good way. His hand's warmth was incredible and felt all of a sudden right and natural after their long day together. Suddenly all of the Christmas decorations seemed endearing and exciting, and she almost asked him to stop for them to take a picture together.

She smiled at him and said, "You're right. I'm glad I checked out Mr. Dorsey's market. He really outdid himself this year. They all did, and now we know where one of the other sleighs went. I wonder if he and Mr. Fournier were the ones who fought over buying the sleigh."

Jake exhaled and glanced at Melissa out of the corner of his eye while he drove slowly through the traffic. His skin glowed in the blinking Christmas lights reflecting in the car and when he smiled, she nearly melted. He squeezed her hand then loosened his grip a bit. Possibly giving her an out, but she didn't take it. She squeezed back, and his grip became firmer and his voice a slight pitch higher.

"Would seem so. I have to give him props on creativity."

The energy bouncing in the car was thrilling. Melissa beamed, staring at their hands as his thumb rubbed lightly back and forth over hers.

"Same. I never would have thought to make Santa out of a giant tomato and have grapes as sleigh bells attached to a grapevine reindeer, and they're all incredibly realistic. They really put a lot of money last minute into their displays. I'm honestly amazed; I never expected this kind of grand exhibit. And to get them done so quickly. Each store front is a great photo opportunity."

Jake glanced at her.

"They took your recommendations to heart. Everyone here knows that you know what you're talking about when planning, and if you suggest something it will turn out amazing."

Melissa felt like a bobblehead from his compliment, but last Christmas flashed before her eyes, ruining the moment.

"I don't know about that. You obviously didn't hear about my big failure last year."

He squeezed her hand. "I read about that, but I also read that it wasn't your fault and that you were basically framed by the governor's personal assistant. I also read that his whole goal was to make your company look bad, and if they lost their most influential event planner then the company would go bankrupt because you practically made the company what it was."

"You read the retraction! I didn't think anyone saw that."

"Of course, I read it. Just because I hadn't talked to you in years didn't mean that when I read something wonderful about you, I didn't think about you. You are a perfectionist and a list master. Those errors had to have been because someone sabotaged you."

Melissa squeezed his hand and turned her head away. She didn't want him to see the few tears that escaped her lids at his kind words.

"Thank you, Jake. That means the world to me."

He squeezed her hand back as he entered the City Hall parking lot, where Melissa had left her car. Jake pulled into the open spot next to her bright yellow Mini Cooper and put his SUV into park. Melissa tried to unclasp their hands, but Jake held on tighter. The atmosphere changed, and Melissa could almost feel the electric charge running through her.

"Lissy?" Jake whispered. Melissa turned to him. His expression changed, the worry line was back, and his Adam's apple bobbed with a deep swallow.

Her heart sank. His expression didn't match the happy feeling of holding hands for the first time. What was he going to say? That he finally realized she was a screw-up, and he couldn't lie anymore, or maybe that holding her hand was a big mistake, or worse brotherly love just like the kiss to the forehead? Was the romantically charged energy she felt all one-sided? She tried to jerk away, to escape before she started crying. She didn't want to hear his rejection, but he wouldn't let her hand go. He held firm and cleared his throat, his voice louder and rushed.

"Would you like to go to dinner with me tonight?"

Melissa stopped struggling to leave and turned back to him flabbergasted. Her fears were wasted. And not knowing how to react anymore, she stared at him like an idiot.

"Lissy?" Jake looked just as freaked out.

Her heart that felt like it stopped only seconds ago began to flutter again like a fleet of hummingbirds trying to break free out of her chest. Without any hesitation she nodded and eventually found her voice.

"I'd love to."

Relief swept through Jake as his body relaxed, and he lifted her hand in his, kissing the back of it.

"Can I pick you up at eight?"

With her mouth full of cotton, she swallowed deeply and replied, "Yes."

Melissa got out of the car with Snickerdoodle in her arms. She wanted to do a jig out of excitement that her dreams from so long ago, of being with Jake, were finally coming to fruition, but she restrained herself and slowly got into her car. When she started her car, he waved, and then he backed out and drove off. She screamed and did a little dance in her seat while Snickerdoodle barked along with her.

After quieting down Melissa turned to Snickerdoodle, petting her on her head.

"Sorry, girl." Snickerdoodle yapped happily, not seeming bothered by her outburst.

"Jenna will flipping freak out when I tell her."

CHAPTER SIXTEEN

M elissa rushed into her room, glad her dad wasn't home yet. She hurried to take a shower, dry her hair, and put her makeup on. When she was done, she FaceTimed Jenna.

"Hey, girl," Jenna answered while holding her nephew on her

shoulder.

Melissa squealed, and the baby's body jolted and he started whimpering.

"Sorry! I have some news!"

The baby was crying now, and Jenna looked frazzled.

"Hold on, let me reposition him."

Melissa stared at Jenna's ceiling fan for a few minutes before her face came back onto the screen.

"Sorry."

"Where's the baby?"

"He was falling asleep before you called. I think I finally got him used to me. He won't take long to go back to sleep."

"I hope that means you'll get some good sleep tonight."

"I probably will, being it's my last day to watch him. Leigh Ann will be coming home tomorrow."

"Wow, I can't believe the week is already over."

"So, tell me your gossip."

Melissa felt like a teenager sitting on her bed talking to Jenna about her crush, and out of habit she started bouncing and squealed again.

Jenna laughed at the same time as she shushed her.

"Sorry," Melissa whispered to the phone, then spilled her news.

"Jake asked me on a date!"

"Holy mother of pearls! He did not!"

"Yes, and he's picking me up at eight. What should I wear? I swear, Jenna, secretly I have been looking forward to this day since I was seventeen years old."

Jenna squealed. She quieted down and turned her head, listening for the baby. "Do you remember the black dress with the red piping I gave you last year?"

"The one I said I would never wear because it was body-hugging?"

"The dress may have been body-hugging on me, but it's formfitting on you; that's why I gave it to you. You're smaller than I am, plus how could I return a designer label when I knew you'd look fantastic."

"Right, and we can't forget there was a no return policy."

"True, true. Regardless, the dress is yours now and you have to wear it, it's totally date material and I promise you Jake's jaw will drop when he picks you up."

Melissa walked to her closet, pulled the dress out, and held it up in front of the mirror. Her hair and makeup were already done.

"Do you really think so?"

"Yes, go put the darn thing on, and change your lipstick to the Love Red No7."

Melissa laid the phone on her bed and heard Jenna's muffled voice.

"Flip the phone to the mirror so I can see what you look like when you're done."

Melissa went back to the bed, picked up the phone.

"I don't know, Jenna."

"Turn the dang phone around, Mel." When she did, Jenna whistled.

"He won't be able to take his eyes off of you."

Melissa glanced at herself in the full-length mirror once more. The black dress hugged every curve she had, her blonde hair was in waves, and the red lipstick matched the piping trim. She felt like a 1940s movie star. Jenna might be right; Jake's jaw might just drop.

She heard the garage door open and close. Her dad and Andrea arrived at the perfect time to take care of Snicker-doodle. She didn't like leaving her alone.

Sitting on the edge of her bed, she slipped on her heels. She had a feeling when her dad saw her all dressed up that he'd get that "I told you so" glint in his eye, and she wasn't sure she was ready for the teasing that would soon follow.

Glancing around her room, searching for where she laid her phone down, she spied it on her dresser next to the red clutch she pulled out to bring. For the first time since moving home, she realized she needed to update her space.

When Melissa moved back, she put her entire apartment into storage and hadn't changed much in this room since college. There were still pictures of her and her ex, Paul, in frames on the shelves. She slid the phone in her clutch, held it under her arm while she grabbed the nearest frame. She couldn't help stare at what she used to think was a happy expression frozen in time.

In the beginning, when she first started dating Paul, she had been relieved to finally have a boyfriend, but when she glanced up in the mirror at her eyes tonight, they were lit up. Her eyes looked bored in the photo with Paul. She placed the photo down and walked to the shelf and studied the others. She took a selfie, studying her eyes in the photo to see if it captured what she noticed in the mirror. Her eyes were bright with excitement, overflowing with long-anticipated desire. None of the photos with Paul expressed anything except friendliness.

She spoke to the picture.

"Poor Paul. Looking back, I don't think I ever really gave you a chance. Six whole years and yet it was so easy to let you go without a thought. I'm horrible."

Guilt at sticking with him out of comfort and routine hit her hard. And that guilt worsened whenever she thought about how they never actually ended their relationship. She looked back at Paul's smiling face.

"You have to know we are done, don't you? It's been a year already, and we haven't had a real conversation in months."

The doorbell chimed through the house. Melissa jumped, dropping the frame. The glass cracked right over Paul, making him barely visible in the photo. She picked the frame up and placed it on the dresser to repair later, and the brief moments of guilt turned to butterflies of anticipation. She glanced in the mirror one last time, adjusting her usually unruly hair, and smoothed it out with her hand. She barely recognized herself. It had been ages since she took this much time and care of herself.

She picked up Snickerdoodle, who had been happily

playing on the floor with a chew toy, and headed down the stairs.

Jake was standing with his back to her. Her dad and Andrea spotted her first, both with big grins on their faces. Jake turned around, and when his mouth slightly dropped open and turned into an appreciative grin, she was glad Jenna talked her into wearing the dress.

He walked up to her and gave her a peck on the cheek.

"You look stunning."

Her cheeks warmed under his heated gaze, and a nervous chuckle slipped out as Snickerdoodle wiggled in her arms.

"I think she's jealous."

"We can't have that, can we." He took the puppy out of her arms and brought her to face-level.

"Snickerdoodle, you look enchanting this evening. Will you be joining us?"

His eyes shifted to Melissa, waiting for a response, but she couldn't seem to find the words. He surprised her with his sudden change of being so outwardly affectionate, a side of him she never noticed, and the discovery made her strangely fall harder for him and uncomfortable at the same time.

Her dad piped up, breaking the silence.

"Of course, you won't be taking the dog on a date. We're the grandparents, bring our girl over here."

Jake complied. Once his back was turned, she caught her dad's eye, and there it was, the glint; soon the teasing would commence.

Only it didn't. Andrea witnessed his change in demeanor, and she placed one hand on his forearm, waited for him to catch her eye, and gave a slight shake of her head. Frank's eyes softened, and whatever teasing he was about to do stopped.

Melissa was just as surprised by that powerful display as

Jake's affection. Not even her mom had been able to stop her dad once he was ready to pick on her, and all it took was one look and a well-placed hand from Andrea, and she shut him down.

She mouthed thank you to Andrea, and she nodded. At that moment, whatever wall Melissa had put up intentionally or unintentionally disappeared, and she walked over, giving her an impulsive hug. When she stepped back, she hadn't realized a tear was in her eye until Andrea pulled a Kleenex out of the box nearby and wiped the corner.

"We can't have your makeup smudged now, can we?" Melissa looked her in the eyes.

"Thank you." She knew the words were pitiful and didn't tell her everything she wanted to say, but she hoped that Andrea, who seemed to be way more intuitive than she gave her credit for, could read her.

Andrea patted and grabbed her hand, squeezing tight, then wiped her own eyes.

"Anytime."

"Did I just miss something?" Frank asked, watching them.

"I'll explain later, dear. You two better leave before you're late for your reservation."

Melissa turned to Jake, "Oooh, where are you taking me?" Andrea did an imaginary zipped lip and everyone chuckled. When Jake didn't respond quick enough, Andrea spit it out excitedly. "Chez François, the little French restaurant in Pineville. It is my favorite and they are known for giving your seat away if you're more than five minutes late."

She gave Jake, who stood behind Melissa, a pointed look.

Jake placed his hand lightly on Melissa's lower back, guiding her out the house.

"Hint taken." Then he turned to Melissa. "Ready?"

She nodded. Melissa was more than ready. Tonight was

the beginning of all of her dreams coming true and her heart was lighter than it had been in years.

CHAPTER SEVENTEEN

"*I* can't believe we're going to Chez François!" Melissa said as Jake helped her into his SUV.

"You've never been?"

"No." She turned to face Jake while he backed out of the driveway. "Have you?"

"Nope, I assumed you liked it because they were catering the wedding. Are you sure you're good with dinner there?"

"Absolutely! I've wanted to go for ages. Since taking over the planning and going over the menu again with Andrea and François on conference calls, I was anxiously awaiting the big day."

"I'm surprised you didn't go taste-testing the minute you got involved in planning. From what I've seen so far, you have a hand in everything. You completely changed the way the lights are hung over the two most-used streets down-town, leading to the traffic circle, where now stands a Gazebo encasing the Christmas tree we picked out. How you got it fully decorated in under 24 hours, I'll never understand."

He turned to her and winked. Melissa grinned and opened her mouth to reply, but Jake interrupted, finishing his praises of her hard work.

"Then you somehow got Christmas music piped into the entire downtown district. I still can't figure out how you talked Wayne into donating all of the sound systems, and I was there when you did it, agreeing right along with you."

"It's magic." Melissa smiled, her heart swelling in pride that he paid attention to all the little details.

"It truly is." As they were driving through Main Street, pride flooded her as she admired her work.

In three days, she was able to find multiple volunteers and paid city workers to get what she wanted done. They passed the park where only days ago her dad asked for her help, now crowded with families. The ice rink was up, and Alex was at a booth selling tickets and handing out ice skates. The rink was strung with lights and in the center was a disco ball creating ever-changing reflected lights on the ice. Jake pointed out the window.

"Yet another example. Can you please explain when you had time to do this?"

"That was all Sarah and Alex Holstead. I saw Alex with his entire hockey league setting the whole thing up. We really are lucky to have a community who works together."

"Indeed, we are," Jake said quietly.

The energy changed. Melissa placed her hand on his knee.

"Hey, you okay?"

Jake grabbed her hand, steering one-handed.

"Just staying here these past six weeks has reminded me how much I miss living here. I'm going to miss Cypressville when I have to go back home."

Melissa sank back into her seat.

"You going home slipped my mind."

"Same here." He brought her hand to his mouth for a kiss. "Let's not let that interfere with our night. You never know what

the night will bring." He turned to her briefly and winked. "Maybe some of your magic is rubbing off on me, and I'll end up staying forever."

Melissa smiled, turned to face out her window. Those few words sent a wave of joy straight to her heart.

"One can only hope."

They arrived at the restaurant thirty minutes away, located in downtown Pineville, the next town over. Melissa glanced at the dashboard clock.

"Perfect timing."

"Might not have been if that cop had pulled me over for speeding. Remind me to be a good boy and follow the road rules on my way back. I don't want to push my luck twice in one night."

They both were laughing when they entered the crowded restaurant, squeezing in between all the well-dressed people holding cocktails and waiting for their tables. The hostess stood at a podium near the bar.

Jake said, "Reservations for Blessing."

"Excuse me?" The hostess appeared confused. "My last name is Blessing. I made a reservation earlier." The hostess looked down at her computer.

"Yes sir, your table is being prepared right now. It will only be a few minutes."

They turned away to make room for the people behind

them when Melissa bumped into someone. The man turned around as Melissa muttered her apologies.

"Melissa, is that you?"

Melissa wanted to sink into the pits of despair. What in the world was Paul, of all people, doing here? He had two drinks in his hand. He raised the glass, getting the attention of a tall, beautiful blonde who made her way in their direction.

Melissa said a silent prayer that the woman was Paul's date. Paul completely ignored Jake and gave her a peck on the lips and a hug once he gave the woman her drink. Melissa was taken aback and froze up.

"Melissa this is Blair; she is an influencer that my firm and I have been sponsoring this past year. We've been a tag team recently searching for the perfect holiday piece. When she mentioned an email invitation requesting her presence to attend an all-expense-paid trip to Cypressville for their festival, I insisted we jump on it. I missed you tremendously and knew this would be perfect. We could actually spend the holiday together again."

Jake's hand dropped from her waist and he stepped back from Melissa the second the words were out of Paul's mouth. Paul took his opportunity to move in. Blair took note and placed a hand on Paul's arm in a possessive way. Melissa couldn't move, her mind racing, trying to figure out how to fix this.

Blair interrupted. "Is this the girl you've been going on about? The one who last year single-handedly embarrassed the governor's wife and insulted her all in one moment?" Blair laughed and turned to Jake. "Can you believe this woman sat the governor's mistress and his wife at the same table then proceeded to serve chicken cordon bleu, his mistress's favorite dish?" Blair laughed haughtily. "If I recall, his wife was vegan along with nearly half the guests. I heard about it from one of my fellow influencers who attended the ball—who went for the sole reason that this was to be the first huge gala serving a vegan-only menu. Boy, was she surprised, disgusted, and offended when the hundred-year anniversary gala, the first to promote animal rights, served meat."

Melissa, humiliated, wanted to cave into herself. She couldn't believe that after a year people still blamed her for the disaster. Yes, she admitted to not double-checking the guest list or seating chart as she normally did; she trusted the governor's personal assistant. Another mistake she couldn't take back, but seriously after all this time she hoped the corrections in the paper explaining the situation would have prevented gossip.

It wasn't her fault the governor's personal assistant was her boss's ex-boyfriend. A man who never got over their breakup. And it wasn't her fault that he lied and fed all the wrong information to her and her team in an effort to sabotage her boss's company, Perfect Planning.

At least the man got the boot when the governor found out his personal assistant was the true saboteur and karma was served in a long court battle.

All Melissa wanted to do was escape that life and never go back. Yet, here she was planning again and being reminded of her tragic failures. Not only in work but in love.

Seriously, the one night she had a chance to redeem her high school errors of being too shy and afraid to tell Jake she liked him is ruined by a boyfriend who doesn't even realize that they aren't together anymore. Could life get any more complicated?

Paul penetrated her deep thoughts that had slowly started spiraling.

"I'll be in Cypressville tomorrow for the contest. I'll pick you up for coffee at nine, and we will go to your favorite coffee shop. It's called Main Street Java, right? It's still there?"

Melissa blinked rapidly. Shocked that things just got worse, Paul asked her on a date. She couldn't find the words to respond and just stared at him then at Blair fuming beside him. Jake stepped to her side. "Our table is ready."

Melissa's eyes burned. Tears threatened to brim over her lids. She blinked a few times to suppress them. Jake's stress line was back in the center of his brow, and his lips thinned in anger. She hadn't seen them like that since graduation when he tried to tell her goodbye once more and she ignored him, her heart already broken, unable to handle the fact she would probably never see him again.

Her heart sank that she was making him angry again. It was all Paul and that influencer Blair's fault. They ruined her perfect night. Her eyes instantly glossed up again but she wouldn't cry in front of everyone, not tonight. She wouldn't let them see how their words and actions could break her.

Jake clasped her hand in his, his warm grip firm and tight. He put his other hand out to Paul.

"Nice meeting you," he said although Melissa had failed to introduce them and nodded to the woman.

Jake pulled her hand harder, yanking her out of her anxietyinduced stupor. In her high heels Melissa tried to keep pace with Jake as he followed the hostess. Paul, oblivious to her being on a date, shouted over the crowd.

"See you tomorrow at nine."

When they were seated, the waiter gave them menus and Jake ordered a bottle of Chardonnay.

Jake sat in the booth across from her, his elbows resting on the table and his hands clasped, his knuckles white from his tight grip. His posture didn't match the romantic atmosphere and the soft lighting. The little candle on the table flickered from his breath when he broke the silence.

"So, are you and Paul an item?"

"No! Absolutely not," Melissa hurriedly answered, not wanting to leave a pause for confusion. "We haven't seen each other in nearly a year. I mean the last time we talked was in a text three months ago, and it was him checking in on us because we had a huge amount of rain, and he wanted to make sure our home didn't flood like some of the surrounding towns."

Jake visibly relaxed.

"So, to be clear, you are not in a romantic relationship with that guy."

"I am completely single."

When the corner of his lip went up at her words, her mood changed from anxiety to happiness in seconds.

Jake placed his hand on top of the table and wiggled his fingers. Then Jake opened his hand palm up on the table, looked Melissa in the eyes, then glanced down at his hand and back to her. She smiled and took the hint and clasped hands with him.

"I like this side of you Jake. I wish I would have known it in high school."

"What side of me?"

"The side of you that is confident in wanting to be close to me, holding my hand, asking me on a date. Being blatantly honest and asking clear precise questions so that there is no room for error. It's all I've ever dreamed about."

"Wait, what?" He leaned forward closer to the table. "I thought you only wanted to be my friend in high school."

Melissa leaned in. Time for her to come clean. She wanted to end this night on a better note. Maybe if Jake knew that there was no competition, and that she was ready for this, then everything that happened in the bar area would be forgotten.

"It's my turn to be honest. I had a crush on you since the

day Mr. Stevens paired us up in class. I don't think I ever stopped loving you, in a way."

His hand loosened but she held his tighter.

"You were and still are so smart and funny, and you always make me feel comfortable even when I want to be mad and stay away from you. I've never had a friend like that except, of course, Jenna, but in this situation, she doesn't count. I was always afraid to tell you for fear you'd run for the hills and I'd lose my best friend, but I ended up doing that anyway, didn't I? When I heard about Molly passing away, I was devastated for you. I want you to know that I wanted to reach out to you, but I didn't know what to do or say, being how I ended our friendship on bad terms. I wish I wouldn't have been so jealous in those days. I possibly could have been friends with the both of you."

She watched Jake's reactions to her words and his creased brow became deeper and deeper. Now that the truth started pouring out of her mouth it felt like a storm erupted and she couldn't stop.

"I'm sorry for prom, jealousy is the culprit, it's why I said all that stuff. I had gone to the prom to finally confront you and tell you that I loved you, but when I saw Molly kiss you, I couldn't breathe. I couldn't be near you anymore. She stole what I wished mine but never was. I was devastated."

Jake sat back, releasing her hand, practically shaking her off of him. Eyes wide, Melissa sat back, worry etched her brow. Jake's lips thinned again and he was breathing heavily out of his nose.

She added, "And now I feel like a jerk and should have kept my mouth closed."

Melissa placed her hands in her lap, looking down at them, her heart racing. Anxiety trying to rise. She blinked back a few tears but it didn't help. They dripped onto her hands. Once more Melissa seemed to find a way to ruin the night, spilling her guts at the wrong place and the wrong time.

She took a few deep breaths, dabbed under eyes with the black cloth napkin.

"I'm sorry. I probably shouldn't have told you that. I don't know what I was expecting."

The appetizers arrived and broke the awkward silence. Jake thanked the waitress.

"Lissy, I wasn't expecting a confession tonight." Jake blew out a breath and the candle in the center of the table flickered again. "I mean, for years I never understood how we could go from being best friends to not at all. You were everything to me back then, but when you abandoned our friendship, I put all my energy from that point on into Molly. Which I'm grateful for because if I would have acted on my feelings for you back then I never would be the man I am today. This physical stuff—Molly loved being close and always having some kind of contact with me—she taught this to me. What you like is something she gave me. I miss it, I miss her, and even though you and I haven't been around each other for years, you're familiar, and it's easy with you."

Melissa digested Jake's words. Her heart ached. He still loved Molly. He was letting her down easy. The only reason he was showing her affection was out of loneliness for his deceased wife and because she was part of his past and familiar. She tried to put on a fake smile.

"It's easy to be with you too. I think I understand."

"Do you?"

She couldn't answer because the waiter showed up for their order. Melissa interrupted Jake before he said anything.

"Jake, this filled me up and we have an early day tomorrow; can we skip the meal?"

Jake put the menu down.

"Sure." He turned to the waiter. "Please bring us the check?"

He pulled out his wallet and had his credit card ready by the time the waiter came back.

The ride home was long and quiet and all hands were kept to themselves. Melissa couldn't wait to get home, crawl in bed with Snickerdoodle, and cry. She hated this season, nothing good ever came with it.

CHAPTER EIGHTEEN

Knocking at her bedroom door woke Melissa, and she groaned. "Leave me alone."

"Paul's here," her dad said through the door.

Melissa barely comprehended his words.

"What?"

When her dad opened the door, Melissa lay in bed, her hair a mess and makeup smudged from crying. Her dad rushed to her side, pushed her over, and sat beside her. The moment he did, her eyes teared up again.

"Sugarplum, what happened?"

She sat up and hugged her dad, resting her head on his shoulder like she did when she was a child and cried.

"I screwed up. I think I told Jake I loved him since forever and that I was jealous of Molly, and Paul was there and acted as if we were still together when I hadn't seen him in almost a year. I'm not sure what to do to make this right. I don't want to lose Jake again."

Her dad patted her on her back, gave her a squeeze then held her shoulders and pushed her back gently.

"Look at me."

Melissa grudgingly lifted her head. Her dad picked up a Kleenex from the bedside table.

"First, you are going to go wash your face and comb your hair. Then you will come downstairs and talk to Paul and set things straight with that man. You cannot continue to lead him on if you are not interested. Now about Jake, that is something altogether different: the ball is in his court. You laid out your feelings. It's up to him to accept them or reject them, but that doesn't give you the option to stay in bed and wallow. Both you and I know wallowing gets us nowhere, and once you're moving again in the world, life has a way of throwing us a curveball. Don't give up hope."

Melissa took a deep breath. Her dad was right; she needed to fix things with Paul. She was a strong, independent woman who could do this. She hugged her dad.

"You're right. Thanks, Dad. I love you."

"I love you too. Now go clean up, and I'll figure out a way to entertain Paul."

He turned to Snickerdoodle, making smoochy sounds to call her over.

"Let's go outside."

Snickerdoodle uncurled herself from the covers and bounded toward Frank with her tail wagging excitedly at those words. Her dad picked the dog up and was almost out of the door, then he turned back to Melissa as she laid back down. She wasn't ready to face the day.

Her dad cleared his throat loudly.

"Hurry up, if you don't mind. I have to pick Andrea up in fifteen minutes. We're taking the influencers on a tour of the Victorian mansion on Stone Road. They are looking forward to the haunted Christmas theme Old Man Stevens did this year for the festival."

"Ugh, you know he's not much older than you, right?"

Frank shook his head.

"That is neither here nor there. Get up!" Melissa sat up.

"All right. All right, all right, I'm up." She threw a pillow at her dad.

Frank caught it with one hand before it hit him and Snickerdoodle and tossed it back on the bed.

"You know I'm glad you took charge of things. I'm amazed and can't get over how you brought this community together and on board in such a short span of time. Everyone is pulling out all the stops for the festival this year. I'm impressed with how fast you're able to work. I'm curious. How'd you talk Old Man

Stevens into it? He's been a recluse for a while now." Melissa laughed.

"You forget—Mr. Stevens was a literature teacher, and he and his wife's favorite holiday book was Dickens's *A Christmas Carol*. They used to read it in the library every year. I used to go to every reading. He is a remarkable voice actor."

She shifted to sitting with her legs criss crossed and started finger-combing some of the knots in her hair.

"I used that to my advantage; I got the entire English department staff and students involved for extra credit and a hefty donation from Mr. Stevens to help buy the school library some e-readers. I suggested to the group of them to make the production as Scrooge-like as possible."

She stopped messing with her hair and a soft smile graced her lips.

"You know," she said, "I haven't seen Mr. Stevens this happy to be involved in something for a long time. I think he was bored. I'm glad they finished it. I'll have to go check it out later today."

Frank closed the door, and Melissa heard him muttering behind it. "Miracle worker."

She smiled then frowned as she got out of bed to face the music of her poor decisions.

Melissa strolled downstairs twenty minutes later. Paul sat alone on the living room couch, stiff as a board with Snickerdoodle on his lap. His hands were as far away from the dog as possible, treating her as if she had some kind of disease. Snickerdoodle took it in stride and slept in a ball on his lap.

Annoyed at his treatment of Snickerdoodle, she couldn't keep the discord from her voice.

"Hey Paul, where's my dad?"

"He had to leave. Get this little rat from my lap and give me a lint brush, will you?"

Melissa glared at him for speaking ill of her sweet puppy and picked up Snickerdoodle, murmuring loving words while she walked to the kitchen utility drawer in search of the lint roller. She turned to Paul, who followed close behind her.

One of the things she never liked about Paul was the way he bossed her around, telling her what to do. Like assuming she would be wanting to go to coffee with him without actually asking and getting a response. She always had to do what he wanted. She had forgotten that about him.

"You could have used your hands and placed her on the floor if you didn't want to hold her.""There is no way I would dirty my hands on that creature."

Melissa fumed and gritted her teeth so hard Paul had to have heard, but he kept going with his ill-mannered words.

"When did you get the dog? I'm surprised you got the animal knowing I never cared for them."

"Andrea rescued her when some meanie tried to dump her because she was the runt of his litter. People who do that should be caught and fined because this little girl is the sweetest puppy ever."

Melissa finished off her statement with Snickerdoodle close to her face and was gifted with puppy kisses. Paul rolled his eyes in disgust.

"I'm sure you'll be able to find another home for her when you move back to the city."

"I'm not moving back and I am keeping Snickerdoodle." Paul completely ignored her response and changed the topic.

"You took longer than expected. We need to leave," he looked at his watch. Blair texted, stating she would meet me at Main Street Java.

Melissa placed Snickerdoodle in the travel tote and walked to the door.

"Blair's coming for coffee?"

A small surge of hope filled Melissa. Maybe she read Paul's signals wrong. Maybe he wasn't just into Blair as a colleague but truly wanting to date her. She hated getting these mixed signals from him. That was how it always was with Paul. She never really knew what he wanted, but somehow they ended up together. He never really even asked her out. It always seemed to be assumed. Neither of them was ever very clear on things. A trait she would soon change. It was refreshing to be with Jake, who was clear and precise in what he wanted. Even when it sucked, at least it was honest.

Paul opened Melissa's car door and answered her question about Blair.

"No, you practically missed our date by sleeping in."

He smoothed her hair when she sat down. She leaned away from his touch. He didn't even notice. Then there was the fact that he didn't really answer her question and basically criticized her for sleeping in for a date she never agreed to in the first place.

Paul walked around the car and got into the driver's seat. He smiled a crooked smile and her level of aggravation rose a notch. Weird, she used to like his smile, but now she couldn't help comparing it to Jake's. Paul's seemed artificial and somewhat detached, whereas Jake's smile showed in his eyes.

Paul kept prattling on.

"At least we can talk on the way there, and I can still treat you to your favorite, vanilla bean."

"That's your favorite. Mine is a mocha latte."

Again, Paul didn't comment. Annoyed at him, she wondered what she had ever seen in him.

"Blair and I are going on a tour of a haunted mansion. You should come."

"I don't know if Blair will want me there. She must have to blog and do other influencer things. I don't want to be in the way."

"You won't. For the life of me, whoever thought of making a haunted mansion for Christmas is nuts. How ridiculous to have something for Halloween this time of year? I don't particularly care for things like this, but Blair is enchanted, so I guess it's a good sign. The mayor must have hired a fantastic event planner to achieve Blair's accolades."

Melissa started to fidget with the radio, grateful she didn't live far from Main Street. One thing was certain after last night: she didn't want Paul or the nasty Blair to know she was the event planner. If they found out she practically reconfigured everything five days ago, Blair would probably blast her for no reason other than to reignite last year's horrors.

Andrea would never forgive her if one of the influencers posted horrible things about the town. Anxiety briefly showed its ugly head at that thought. She would have to play along with Paul and whatever he thought their thing was until after the wedding, so that Blair can finish all her posts.

She won't let her failed relationship or career get in the way of saving Cypressville's future economy.

Paul guided her in, greeted Walter with a handshake over the counter, and placed the order for two vanilla bean lattes. Walter lifted his brow in question. She mouthed mocha latte. Once more, Paul attempted to get into her personal space, placing his arm over her shoulder. She conveniently bent down to place Snickerdoodle's tote on the ground.

"You are not taking that animal out of the bag in this establishment," Paul said in disgust.

"Snickerdoodle's always welcome in here," Walter piped up.

And he pulled out a cup and squirted it full of whipped cream, handing it to Melissa with a conspiratorial wink.

Fortunately for Melissa, Paul's phone rang.

"Excuse me for a moment; it's the office." He walked out.

"So—you and Paul back together?" Walter had no reservations about butting in.

Melissa's shoulders slumped. "No, I thought we broke up when I moved back a year ago, but I don't think he realizes it."

"Honey, that ain't good. You need to be blunt with him. Some men are slow and can't see beyond the tip of their nose." "So it seems."

"Was that Paul who just walked outside?" Jenna's voice blurted out behind Melissa, startling her.

"It is."

"Girls, can you take your conversation to the end of the counter? Sadly, I have work even though I would love to gossip with you both."

Jenna giggled as they moved.

"Don't worry, Walt. I'll fill you in later."

Jenna pouted then leaned over the end counter.

"I didn't get to place my order."

A large group of people were placing orders with Walter. He leaned back a little and shouted to Jenna.

"Honey, you order the same thing three times a day. I ain't senile yet. I'll have it ready for you." Jenna blew Walter a kiss.

"You're the best."

Walter's cheeks turned all rosy.

Jenna turned to Melissa and put her hand on her hip.

"I leave you alone for one night." She held her forefinger up. "One night, Melissa, and somehow chaos ensued. What the heck is going on, and why is Paul, of all people, here getting coffee with you and not Jake?"

Melissa's body sagged so much that she thought she might melt into the ground.

"I totally screwed everything up. You were right. I wasn't ready to talk to Jake. However, I didn't freeze up, as you expected. I did something way worse. I blurted out in gory detail how much I loved him or used to."

She shook her head and rubbed her temples.

"I can't remember now, it's all a blur, and I think I may have told him I didn't like Molly. On top of that, Paul was at the restaurant, and he somehow still has the delusion that after a year of me living away, I am still his girlfriend and that I will be moving back to the city soon, and he told me to get rid of Snickerdoodle. He's insufferable and won't listen."

Jenna made a low whistle through her teeth.

"Girl, only you can somehow screw things up this royally."

"Thanks, you're a bunch of help," Melissa said sarcastically and slightly miserably at the same time.

"Sorry, but it's the truth." Jenna gave a half-grin,

The bell to the coffee shop dinged, and in walked Blair followed by Jake, who had graciously held the door open for her.

Paul returned without her noticing. His hand gripped

Melissa's waist firmly, making her jump, then he kissed her. It wasn't a big kiss, just a peck on the lips but it was still a kiss. A kiss in front of everyone. She watched Jenna's eyes bounce from Paul to her to Jake and back to her again. Melissa stood frozen, furious and horror-struck. Now Jake would think she was lying about not dating Paul. Jake gave her the most pained expression she had ever seen in her life.

Paul smiled crookedly, stepping away from Melissa to get his coffee order. Jenna hurriedly whispered in Melissa's ear.

"I think Paul staking his claim on you, and if you want a chance with Jake you need to tell Paul it's over today."

Jenna was right. Melissa witnessed Jake's hands ball up at his sides, and his eyes turned from pained to complete ice. He turned around and left before he even fully made it into the shop. Melissa fought the urge to cry and whispered back to Jenna.

"I know I have to tell him we're done, but I can't today. There is too much at stake with the festival. You haven't heard the worst of last night. Blair knows about the governor's ball; she practically attacked me with her vicious knowledge at the restaurant last night. I can't screw things up for Andrea. Paul and Blair can't

find out at all costs that I'm the event planner." Jenna squinted her eyes.

Melissa whispered back. "Don't give me that look."

"What look?"

"The one that says this is a bad idea. I'll tell him eventually. All at the right time."

"You better, but I still think you should stop procrastinating and be honest."

"No, I can't."

Jenna rolled her eyes and muttered into her cup.

"You might lose Jake again."

"Shut up." Melissa moaned in hushed tones. "Seriously,

stop. I can't think like that. I'll figure something out," she said as Blair came up to her and acted as if they were long-lost fake friends.

Blair gave Melissa an air kiss on each cheek.

"Melissa, so good to see you again."

Melissa and Jenna gave each other the "what the heck was that?" look. Then Blair grabbed Paul's hand and pulled him toward her.

"Paul and I are just heading out to the Haunted Christmas Mansion, so sorry we won't be able to chat." Jenna mouthed to Melissa, "She likes him." Blair had her nose in the air.

"Come along, Paul, we don't want to be late."

Blair glared at Melissa when Paul placed his hand back on her waist and leaned in to her.

"Let's grab our coffee and go." He then looked at Jenna. "Would you like to come along?

Blair's shoulders stiffened. She applied a fake smile as if it were makeup and turned around, ignoring them all, and walked out briskly. Paul actually noticed something was wrong with Blair.

"I wonder what upset her?" He walked off, following her.

Jenna finished adding her cream and sugar to her coffee, capped it, and smiled mischievously. "I wouldn't miss it for the world."

CHAPTER NINETEEN

As the four of them arrived her dad and Andrea stood on the sidewalk next to the wrought iron gate leading to the estate. Andrea was speaking to the crowd of influencers and their guests. The tour was about to start. Her dad lifted his right brow in question, and Melissa shrugged, shook her head, and gave him sad eyes.

Her dad's mouth turned down in disappointment. Andrea nudged Frank with her elbow.

"Right." He opened the gate. "After you." When Melissa was near him, he whispered, "Don't let this go on too long, Mel."

She didn't have time to explain why she was waiting before her dad jogged back to Andrea's side. Fifteen different influencers stood around Mr. Stevens's front door. Each one taking a turn with their selfie sticks and friends, family, or sponsors posing with them in front of the large door knocker that eerily resembled the one from the old movie. The chatter as each spoke into their phones buzzed in her ears like a swarm of bees.

Blair immediately got to work, pulled out her selfie stick,

and placed her phone in the holder. She turned around and posed with her fingers in a peace sign and the beautiful Victorian house in the background. Then she grabbed Paul, and they took one together when it was their turn at the door knocker. Mr. Stevens even had suspenseful music like in the movies playing in the background, making it seem like something was coming.

Paul was actually laughing, and his eyes were bright and cheery. He and Blair looked fantastic together, and a plan started brewing inside her head. Melissa turned to Jenna. "I have an idea."

"You look like the cat who ate the cream. What's going on inside that brain of yours?"

"I'm going to get Paul and Blair together, then he'll forget all about me, and my problem will be solved."

"Seriously, Mel, I don't think that's a good idea. You need to tell him."

"No, listen, she obviously likes him. Every time he is with me, she always touches him or tries to bring his attention back to her when he's near me. Didn't you notice her expression when he said you and I were coming? In a matter of seconds, her features went from fury, to disappointment, to a fake smile of tolerance. Help me put them together."

"All right, but mark me in the books as telling you I think it's a bad idea."

Melissa gave Jenna a hug.

"Noted."

This had to work. She had to prove to Jake that she and Paul were over, and this way it would be a win-win. Paul would like Blair and Jake would see Paul wasn't into her anymore.

Paul was back at Melissa's side as soon as the photos were done; they were at the back of the group and Paul seemed hyped up.

"Blair loves Dickens and explained to me this is no ordinary haunted house but a live-action version of *A Christmas Carol*. It should be interesting. The more I think about it, your mayor is a genius. She must have done her research because, according to Blair, every activity so far is ticking off the list of the perfect Christmas, but this is the pièce de résistance so far. She has been to plays of course but never has she been to a live-action portrayal of Scrooge such as this."

"Wonderful. Hopefully, she will have nothing but praise for our little festival."

Melissa hurried away from Paul, aiming to catch up with Blair. Perfect time to put her plan into action. Blair appeared exhilarated to be here for the tour, and Paul was singing her praises.

Blair scrunched her brow when Melissa walked beside her but immediately turned to the first room, where Ebenezer and Bob Cratchit were sitting in the office freezing, and Bob was asking about being off for Christmas. The room was actually cold and Melissa shivered.

Blair turned to Melissa with a genuine smile. "This is fantastic." Her camera clicked away.

"I'm glad you think so. Paul was telling me how much he admired your work and that this is your first time blogging about

a live-action retelling of *A Christmas Carol*." Blair blinked rapidly three times.

"He was?"

"Yes."

Melissa paid close attention to Blair's body language. Her shoulders dropped a notch and her eyes softened, tilting up in the corners slightly. Blair immediately squinted her eyes at Melissa, turning away without another word toward the next room.

Melissa followed and tried again. She could tell Blair

wanted to believe her. This was her sign of hope. This time she tried a different tactic. One about the house and maybe a little extra plug for the kids and staff who worked hard on making this project come together in such a short time.

"Mr. Stevens, the owner, decided at the last minute to open his house for tours. Years ago, his wife and him would have a huge open house party for the town. Since his wife passed, he hadn't had the heart to open it but this year he decided it was a time for change. He, along with the mayor's event planning committee, contacted the principal of McKinley High. The entire Language and Arts department staff and all the students worked day and night to help recreate Scrooge in only four days. It turned out wonderful so far, don't you think?"

"*A Christmas Carol*," Blair corrected. She started walking to the next room and for a moment Melissa nearly gave up her plan. But after Blair turned, looking into the next room, her face lit up and she finally opened up.

"They did a phenomenal job. The first few scenes were great. The Jacob Marley in handcuffs and jail costume was a comical take on him being imprisoned by his greed. I'm looking forward to their interpretation of the first ghost."

Relief swept through Melissa as they watched Scrooge go to sleep and the bells chime as the Ghost of Christmas Past appeared, walking out of Mr. Stevens's armoire dressed in a pixie costume with fairy lights wound around her head like a crown.

Blair whispered, "Adorable."

Melissa needed to befriend Blair enough to get in her good graces, hoping that she would confide in her and open up about her feelings for Paul. Melissa plastered on her best smile. "You know, Blair, I've been thinking... If you'd like, I can get the mayor to give you a one-on-one interview with her and the actors. Mr. Stevens, the homeowner, is playing Ebenezer. I'm sure he wouldn't mind giving you a tour also; his house is the oldest house in our community, dating back to 1896."

Melissa crossed her fingers behind her back, hoping she didn't cross the boundaries of her profession and as a human. What was she turning into just because she couldn't face Paul with the truth? But Blair's eyes widened and she placed her hand on Melissa's arm.

"I would love that."

Melissa's disgust in herself fled. She was shocked her plan was working. Genuine excitement graced Blair's presence until her smile wavered.

"Why are you looking at me like you're in shock or something?" Blair's eyes turned shrewd and she bombarded her with question after question. "What's this about? What are you after? Why me out of all of the influencers?"

Melissa stumbled with her words, mad at herself for not being a good actress.

"Well—Paul's an old friend. I haven't seen him in almost a year, and it seems like he's really into you, and if you're important to him and his company, I want to help."

That sounded like a good excuse that would hopefully help her cause.

Blair sniffed the air, her expression tight, and turned and walked to the next room.

"Fudge."

Melissa trailed after Blair. How did she take that the wrong way? While ruminating on what she said, she took in the next room. The long dining room table was set up with china and silver candelabras and a long, lace tablecloth. The serving dishes were laden with fruits and meats piled high. The fragrance was amazing and her stomach actually growled.

Mr. Stevens wore a long white nightgown and had on a

winter glittery white snow cap with a hot pink pompom on the end. Melissa had to cover her mouth to prevent the giggle from coming out. Sylvia Taylor, who couldn't be more than five feet tall, played the Ghost of Christmas Past and was standing in the center of the table pointing a glow-in-the-dark wizard's wand at Ebenezer, explaining to him where they were in his past.

When they left that room, Blair's demeanor changed once more, and interpreting her body language was becoming exhausting. This time Blair wasn't fake friendly or excited about the house; she was calculating and blunt.

"Just to confirm I understood you correctly. I would be the only influencer to have this exclusive interview, or is this some sort of plan to make your town look good, or is this some plot the mayor concocted to get the town's sweet little golden child to sneak into the good graces of each influencer for better reviews?"

Melissa immediately backed up and put her hands up to diffuse the hostility in Blair's words, and she backpedaled in an effort to rectify her horrible plan to get Blair to like her. Melissa's anxiety grew.

"Oh my gosh. No! You have it all wrong." She blathered out in a rush. She grabbed Blair's forearm. "You have to believe me," Blair shook her off and Melissa scrambled to think of what to say. "I really only wanted to get to know you, I was hoping to get Paul to see how amazing you are. I want him to see in you what I see."

Blair's eyes blazed. "What did you say?"

Melissa freaked out; her plan was crumbling away before her eyes and she almost accidentally told Blair her plan. She ignored her question and prattled on.

"I promise it's only you and I'll talk to Mayor Jackson immediately to make sure she knows it's only you."

Blair wiped her forearms as if where Melissa touched had cooties. She then plastered on a fake smile, her eyes cold.

"Yes, that would be perfect. Now, if you don't mind, I'd like to enjoy the rest of this on my own. Your presence is starting to ruin this event for me."

Melissa stood still for a moment, her heart pounding hard in her chest. Blair caught up with the rest of the group. When Melissa spotted Jenna two people away from Blair, she gave her a watery smile and Jenna mouthed, "I told you so."

Melissa scanned the small crowd for Paul but couldn't find him. But she didn't have to wait long. He came up from behind her seconds later, making her jump as he wrapped his arm around her shoulder.

"Thanks for waiting for me."

Melissa stooped down and out of his grasp instantly and walked a few steps ahead of him, trying to hurry and catch up to the group.

"Where did you come from?"

"I was behind you and Blair the whole time; it looked like you wanted to be alone with her so I dawdled. What were you and Blair talking about?"

"Basically, how I would get her a private interview with the mayor and actors after the tour. I was hoping it would help boost her blog over the other influencers' and help your company."

Paul grabbed her shoulders, stopping her, spun her around and once more before she had time to think what he was doing he stunned her by kissing her right there in front of everyone. Her eyes wide in shock, her lips sealed tight and closed, she immediately searched the crowd to see who was witness to this public display. Of course, it was Blair whose cheeks were red and blotchy and her eyes shot daggers at Melissa from across the hallway. Then she noticed Jenna who just shook her head. Melissa felt Jenna's disappointment in her in that one motion and her eyes burned in shame.

Her only saving grace was that Jake wasn't there to witness it again. Paul's words broke through her litany.

"You are brilliant. Thank you for helping with my sponsorship. I knew if I came with Blair, you'd help me out. That is what love is about, after all, right?"

Melissa had to hold her tears in; her plan backfired. Jenna was right, and all it took was less than a half-hour to prove it. The rest of the tour was a blur, but she made it to her dad's side with Paul still trailing behind her. She had pulled Snickerdoodle out of her tote that she was sleeping in and held her close for comfort and hopefully to keep Paul away.

She stomped her way over to her dad and the mayor. It was time to face the consequences of her actions. She had to talk to Andrea and her dad and let them know her worries and fears of breaking it off with Paul and get their advice. This couldn't go on any longer. She also needed to explain to Jake why this was all happening. She was already honest with him once and even if he didn't want to see her ever again, she had to explain. She wouldn't let another ten years go by on misunderstandings and lies.

CHAPTER TWENTY

Jake stormed into Susan's shop, taking his frustration out on the first box he spotted. First their date got cut short and didn't go as he planned, but he thought it was all worked out and she was ready to be with him. Now, she was getting all cozy in the coffee shop with the man she said she was done with. Reaching into the box, he ripped off the protective wrap from the next items and started placing them aggressively on the shelf.

Susan scootered her way over to him.

"What has your tinsel all knotted up this morning?"

Jake gave her the stink eye.

"What?"

"Why are you charging in here like a bull in a china shop? You left home not even an hour ago, more chipper than a Christmas elf in tights, and now you're behaving like the Grinch."

Jake stopped putting things on the shelf. "What I thought — was wrong. Now I have to reassess."

Susan rolled her eyes at Jake. "Well, that sure is cryptic."

Jake leaned against the solid oak table behind him. It displayed an ornament tree hanging various mistletoe balls. All he could think about when looking at those darn balls was Melissa's lips. Then the image of her lips touching Paul's popped into his head, and his anger rose. It should have been him kissing her, not Paul. He sighed and stood up again and picked up another box. Susan made an obnoxious clearing of her throat when he was rough with it, so he gently finished opening the box.

He unwrapped a miniature Santa statue and placed the figurine on the shelf across from the table. After a few minutes he noticed Susan wasn't leaving. She stood there dusting each figurine he placed on the shelf, patiently waiting for him to talk.

"I don't want to talk about it. The grand opening is tomorrow, and we have a lot left to do."

"That's true."

Susan gave him a long look then thankfully took the hint and went back to decorating the Christmas tree in the center of the store. Two ornaments in, she hollered across the store, "Where's my coffee?"

Jake practically growled as he dropped the empty box to the floor. He squashed the box, stomping on it several times, pretending it was Paul's head. He grabbed the flattened box, stormed to the back of the store, and threw it in the trash pile by the back door with the other compacted boxes.

He sat heavily in the chair, rested his elbows on the desk, and put his head in his hands. What was wrong with him? He was never this jealous over anyone in his entire life. He understood a relationship with Melissa might not work. After all, he would be leaving right after Christmas. But after reading her book, the ideas about going freelance started becoming a real plan.

He started making contacts and getting elements in order

with his CPA to form his own business. Melissa was an amazing writer, and he wanted to propose not only being her editor but also her literary agent. He was certain he could sell her book.

Visions of them starting a life together were turning into a reality. Or at least it was beginning to when he asked her on the date. The entire night turned into a disaster, destroying his dreams in a moment.

Her confession of love threw him for a loop. He had no idea she had loved him back in school, and she implied she still did. Or was that his own hopes? Regardless of if she did or didn't, when she allowed Paul to kiss her this morning after her confession last night, the intensity of pain and betrayal was like a lightning bolt to his heart.

He didn't have the guts to face her, to listen to her excuses. Were her words the night before just lies? How could he trust her? Didn't she lie before? What would make her not lie to him again?

Susan's hand rested on his shoulder, making him stiffen slightly.

"Jake, what's going on?" Susan's soft voice was filled with concern.

He placed his head in his hand, and his voice was barely a whisper.

"Sue, I was a fool to let myself dream again." Susan spun his chair around toward her.

"Jake." She breathed out. "No, you aren't. It's okay to be happy and feel again. Megan loves this new playful happy version of you; it's all she can talk about these days, and she loves every second of your newfound Christmas spirit. And if Melissa is a part of this change, I am happy."

"But I'm confused. I think Lissy is still dating a man named Paul. He is in town, and even though she seemed surprised to see him last night and told me they were not together and she was totally single—this morning in the coffee shop they were kissing." Susan sat down on her knee scooter.

"Wait, her ex-boyfriend is in town?"

"Yes, he is sponsoring an influencer who seems to dislike Lissy. She was a right witch last night bringing up Lissy's event planning disaster last year."

"Poor Melissa, she must have been in shock. She has had a rough two years. After her momma died, she struggled with being away from her dad, and when the disastrous event happened, she came home with her tail between her legs. She didn't leave the house much until recently." Jake looked up at Susan.

"You knew about all of this."

"Of course. How could I not? I worked for the mayor until recently and Andrea and I are friends. Why wouldn't she talk to me about her future daughter."

"So, Paul really is her ex?"

"As far as we all know. Melissa wasn't very forthcoming in conversations with Andrea. There are many complications in their relationship. The main one—she found out her dad and Andrea were engaged from Walter. He thought she knew, since Jenna told him and congratulated her on her father's upcoming nuptials. Andrea told me Frank postponed telling her because he was worried about how she'd take the news, being it had only been a year since her mom's passing. He wanted to plan the perfect time. The delayed news and the gossip chain destroyed his plan and put up a barrier between them for a while. Andrea told me Melissa tends to hold her heart inside her chest and has so many walls protecting it that it would take an army to break her. But what we do know as fact is Paul hasn't been around these parts in nearly a year. The last time was Thanksgiving before she moved home. When she came here, not once did Paul come. She never spoke of him, and when her dad asked if he was coming for Easter, she said they broke up. At least that's what I know."

Jake sat back after listening to this new insight into Lissy. He had a lot to think about, and he had to figure out his emotions by tonight. He was supposed to meet her for the gingerbread contest, and he couldn't let his feelings for her interfere in Megan's first contest. She was looking forward to it.

He said, "Tonight is the gingerbread contest. Are you coming?"

Susan stood up and patted Jake on the shoulder.

"I wouldn't miss it for the world. I can't believe you promised to help Megan build a house tonight, especially after the last time you entered the contest. They banned you and Melissa from the event altogether."

He smiled at Susan. "That was a long time ago. We've grown up since then, and Lissy and I made a pact we would show the town and Megan what a winning gingerbread house looks like. We have a plan."

"Oh no! I'll need to prepare a bath for Megs when she gets home. I have a feeling she will be covered in icing. I'll never forget Mom's face when you walked in covered in red and green icing. Didn't it stain your skin for a couple of days?"

Jake laughed. "I completely forgot about the staining of our skin. Lissy and I were the talk of the town that weekend. We looked like we got caught in some type of icing explosion."

Susan shook her head at him. "I really need to go now to keep all three of you in line."

"Very funny. I doubt we will be up to no good this time. We have to do our best to win for Megan, but I would love for you to come. Maybe it will help it feel less awkward."

"I'll be there then, with jingle bells on."

CHAPTER TWENTY-ONE

$\mathcal{M}$elissa spotted Andrea and her dad after the performance, speaking to a few of the influencers in the back garden. Teenagers dressed in elf costumes served refreshments. Blair stood nearby on one of the iron patio sets stirring her hot chocolate with a peppermint stick, giving her evil eyes.

Paul was right behind Melissa, gently shoving her.

"There's the mayor; let's go and get this private interview set up."

"Paul, stop pushing me."

Paul stopped shoving her then walked around her and went up to her dad.

"Frank, great show, man. You and the mayor put on a wonderful program. Your event planner must be top notch. Who is it?"

Frank opened his mouth to speak and Melissa was frantically signaling him behind Paul's back not to answer.

"Well, now, um, we're keeping the planner's name hush-hush. Don't want anyone to—"

Paul didn't let her dad finish and turned to the mayor

with his hand extended. "Not sure we've had the pleasure of meeting. I am Paul Donaldson, Melissa's fiancé. She told me you would be delighted to give Blair a private interview with yourself and the cast of this lovely performance."

Melissa was flabbergasted. Her mouth hung open in complete shock. Andrea shook his hand, her eyes widened briefly, but being the professional she was, she didn't miss a beat.

"Of course, we'd be honored to have Blair do a showcase piece. She will of course be posting to all of her social media platforms by this evening, correct?"

"Absolutely." Paul agreed. "As I'm sure you all are aware, Blair is by far one of the most followed influencers at your town's festival. Her reviews and posts will gain more traction. By Christmas this place will be packed."

"Well, Paul, I am sure you are aware Christmas is five days away and tomorrow is the Christmas tree lighting. Now that is the event we are hoping to have jam-packed. If you can guarantee her attracting the attention of fifty or more new tourists into town by tomorrow then we have a deal. Tell Blair to have each person who watches her post drop her name on the back of their business card in different stores around town. It will enter them into a grand prize drawing being held tomorrow to win a weekend stay at one of our local B&Bs. And tell them to stay for the tree lighting; they will all be in for a huge surprise."

Melissa was stunned Andrea hinted at her wedding and mouthed "thank you" to Andrea, but her anger over Paul's nerve to weasel his way to the mayor was beyond redemption. Melissa couldn't believe his gall. Never in all the years she dated Paul did they ever talk about marriage or him propose to her. This had to stop, no matter what happened to the festival. Her dad and Jenna were right, Paul would destroy her chances with Jake and she wouldn't let it continue. Melissa stepped forward angrily. "Paul, I need to have a word with you."

She tugged his sleeve and practically yanked him away from her dad and Andrea. "What the heck, Paul? You and I are not engaged. We never have been and—"

The jerk had the audacity to laugh. "I know, but if she thought we were engaged then for sure she would do the interviews. Who would have thought this would turn out so well? Only fifty tourists, what a piece of cake. By the time Blair posts her interview at least a few hundred tourists will be lining up to visit this town."

"Well, I'm certainly glad you have faith in Blair. But seriously Paul, you do know I live with my dad? He knows we aren't engaged. I mean you and I have barely seen each other in a year. We aren't even dating anymore, and by the way around Blair I got the feeling you were into her. I can totally see she's into you.

Why aren't y'all dating?"

For the first time all morning, Paul shut up. He stood there like a statue for a few seconds. "Did you say Blair is interested in me?"

"Is that all you heard? Yes, I think the girl might actually be in love with you the way she gives me angry eyes every time you touch me. Don't tell me you never noticed."

"I haven't. Honestly, you know me. I'm not the type of guy who stops enough to pay attention. I think I was too focused on you and seeing you again to think about Blair in any other way than the woman our company sponsors."

"Paul, did you think we were still dating? I mean, we haven't talked in ages. Shouldn't that have been a clue that we fizzled out?"

"Of course. We never really dated to begin with though, did we? You and I developed a camaraderie with the benefits of being the plus-one for each other on special occasions and events. I never thought it needed explaining, and you never asked for more. I guess I assumed you and I were on the same page."

Melissa's ego dropped into her shoes. It sucked. For nearly six years, her relationship with Paul was mostly an afterthought or a plus-one, but at the same time she never invested her whole self into Paul either. Maybe in the beginning she gave a little but over the last few years he'd been an afterthought to her as well.

She lifted her shoulders, deciding it was good he felt that way. This way there would be no hard feelings and Blair would still make a good post. Her fears earlier were for nothing.

"Well, Paul, I don't think Blair would like to be thought of as your plus-one girl. She seems more like the I-want-a-fairytalewedding sort of girl, and if I'm honest that's the kind of girl I am too but just not with you. No offense."

"None taken."

Paul gave her a hug and she stiffened up. He pulled back. "I guess this is goodbye." Melissa nodded.

He stuffed his hands in his jacket pockets. "I won't stand in the way or give the other guy mixed signals again. Sorry I did it to begin with but I have to admit that was the first time you showed interest in someone besides me. I knew our time was over but I wasn't quite ready to admit it all of a sudden."

She accepted his apology with a nod. "Goodbye, Paul. Thanks for understanding."

He started walking away and then turned around, giving her his crooked smile. "Thanks for the heads-up on Blair."

Paul turned back around and started whistling as he walked toward Blair. When he got to her, he must have told her they got the interview because she hugged him and squealed like a schoolgirl. It was strange to see Blair in a different light. They looked good together. Paul pulled his hands out his pockets and returned her hug. Probably the first time he ever gave the girl any type of affection. Hopefully they would work out their relationship. Now it was Melissa's turn to apologize to Jake again and try to start hers.

Melissa and Jenna sat at a small two-seater table crammed in the back office/breakroom of Jenna's monogram shop. They had picked up lunch from the local bakery and Melissa held her phone in her hands, her finger hovering over the send button.

"Just press send, Mel. You need to get this over with."

"I'm nervous. What if he doesn't respond? I mean how will I act tonight when we have to meet up for the gingerbread contest?"

"You'll never know until you send the message," Jenna said before taking a bite of her sandwich.

"I don't know. Maybe the message is too long. Some of this should probably be told face to face."

Jenna groaned and plucked the phone out of Melissa's hands so fast Melissa didn't have time to grab it back before Jenna pressed the send button.

"There. Now you have nothing to contemplate anymore. Done. Now it's all up to Jake."

Melissa slumped back in her chair, arms across her chest, her sandwich still in its wrapper.

"Stop your pouting and eat. I only have—" Jenna glanced at the digital clock blinking on top of the counter where the small ironing board sat. "Ten more minutes before I need to open the shop back up."

Melissa took a bite of her sandwich and nearly choked

when her phone dinged. She swallowed the lump of the sandwich down hard and, with trembling hands, picked up her phone.

She took a deep breath and held the phone to her heart, then pulled it forward and sent a short text back.

"Girl, you better not leave me hanging. What did he say?"

"He wrote, 'See you tonight.'"

"That's all? Those three words have you hugging your phone as if he told you he loved you."

Melissa felt her cheeks warm at Jenna's word.

"That may not seem like much to you, but this means he's still willing to talk to me. After prom, I screwed up. Too young, too hurt, too prideful. I don't want to be that girl anymore. I want to be honest with Jake. If all I get is him as a friend or possibly a business partner with my writing, I'll be okay with it. I don't want to lose him again."

"But?"

"But what?"

"Mel, there has to be a but. You have to want to date the man. I know you. You will never be content with just friends, especially if he brings another woman into his life."

Melissa finished her sandwich, crumpled her wrapper, stood up, and picked up the remains of Snickerdoodle's food as well and dropped them both in the trash by the door. Scooping the sleeping puppy up and placing her gently in her tote, she turned around to Jenna.

"I don't want to talk about this anymore."

"Deflecting much?" Jenna grumbled from her spot at the table.

Melissa leaned against the door frame leading to the monogram station. "Come on, Jenna, let me have this moment without psychoanalyzing my poor history and future with Jake. I need to feel confident in this decision."

"That's my point, Mel, you aren't comfortable with it, and

you need to face the facts and yourself. You have to accept that you may never date him and that the idea you have in your head of you and Jake is a fantasy. Real life is not a romance story or happily ever after. If it were, then we would all have these epic love stories to tell everyone. Love just happens."

"Oh, is that so? Where is your love, Jenna? I don't see you falling for anyone."

"Because I haven't met him yet. When I meet him, I promise love will happen easily with none of this up and down stuff. Look at your dad and the mayor. They were working together, and love happened. It happened the same way with my parents and, if I'm not mistaken, with your dad and mom too. That is what you should be looking for, something that is easy and develops gracefully into companionship, not all this heartache and trying to fix problems."

"Thanks for the lecture on how you define love, but I'm outta here. I have a meeting with Andrea and need to check on the final details of the wedding for tomorrow night."

Jenna walked behind Melissa and grabbed her arm to stop her. "Hey."

Melissa clenched her teeth and gave Jenna an exasperated look. "What?"

Jenna frowned and within seconds was hugging the stiff-armed Melissa and whispering in her ear. "I'm sorry. You're right. I have no room to talk. I don't want you to get hurt, and I'm being overprotective of your heart, but it's yours to do as you wish." She stepped back. "Forgive me?"

"Of course. We're BFFs. You're always forgiven." Melissa gave her a small smile.

They hugged again. This time Melissa hugged Jenna back and headed out to Main Street.

CHAPTER TWENTY-TWO

$\mathcal{M}$elissa paused, watching the traffic flow, and waved to a few of the influencers she had seen previously around town shopping. It was hard to believe how a few posts could bring in this many people to their small community. She headed over to City Hall for her meeting with Andrea.

Opening the door, the atrium was packed with staff placing tables and chairs in the appropriate places. Melissa found Cheryl in the center of the room, surrounded by boxes of flowers and vases.

"Hey Cheryl, the setup for the reception is coming along great. Thanks again for supervising the setup for me."

Cheryl lifted her head, looking frazzled. "Oh, Melissa, hey."

"Everything all right? You look a bit lost."

Cheryl placed the flowers in her hand on the table. With her head tilted down, she laid her hands flat on the surface. When she lifted her head, she had tears in her eyes.

"I screwed up all of the arrangements. I told you I could handle ordering the flowers and—" She waved her hand to all of the boxes around her full of fake silk blue and gold blooms of some of the most unappealing flowers Melissa had ever seen. "This is what arrived. I don't know how I made this big of a mistake, but I should have known it was too good to be true when the price came in well below what you told me I should expect."

Melissa walked over to the box and picked up one of the flowers with a wilting fake petal. *How do fake petals even wilt?* she wondered as she picked up the fake glitter-sparkling berry with parts of the white Styrofoam still showing. She turned to the crying Cheryl.

"Don't worry, we can make this work. I need you to go to the arts and craft store in Pineville and buy a few things that will make this work."

"I don't think you should trust me with this. I have never been crafty. I'll probably end up picking the wrong thing again."

"No, you won't. I will find the stuff on the website and text you the pictures. All you will need to do is have the associate working there help you find the product." Melissa grabbed Cheryl's hands. "We will make this work. Don't worry. By the time you and I are done with this, you will be a pro."

Cheryl gave Melissa a watery smile and wiped her eyes with a Kleenex she pulled out of her pocket.

"Thank you for being so understanding. I would have been furious if one of my staff made this big of a mistake, and not only that, I was so scared that the mayor would find out before I could get your help. I've been hiding from her all morning."

Melissa laughed. "Well, we can't let her find you or these flowers yet." She pulled out an expense card from her purse and gave it to Cheryl. "Go on and go. I have to meet Andrea for our final meeting before tomorrow's big day. I'll keep her busy so she won't come pestering you here."

Cheryl put the card in her slacks pocket. Her shoulders lifted as if a weight had been lifted off.

"Thanks. I'm excited. I'll have to get used to calling her Mayor Albright."

"That will be a definite change but for the good."

As Cheryl headed off to take care of that unexpected problem, Melissa covered all the boxes and headed to Andrea's office to meet with the seamstress, who was kind enough to meet them at the office to do the final fitting.

Since the festival started, Andrea had been spread so thin with her time going from event to event with the influencers that this was the only time there was to spare for the final fitting and for Melissa to explain the idea for Andrea's grand entry.

The door to the office was open.

"Knock, knock."

Andrea had closed all of the window blinds and was surrounded by hanging racks and boxes of shoes, gloves, and veils. "Oh, thank goodness you are finally here. Look at all of this stuff that was delivered today. I thought this was my last fitting."

Melissa placed her tote on the nearest chair, picked Snickerdoodle up out of her tote, kissed her head then placed her on the floor to wander around the office. Melissa walked over to one of the boxes and pulled out a pair of above elbow white silk gloves.

"These will look beautiful with your complexion and pop with your red dress."

"Gloves? Really? I am not the princess type, Melissa. I am the go-getter business type."

"Andrea, tomorrow night you're getting married. For one night in your life, you need to be the princess. No, scratch that. You need to be the queen that you are. You will be stunning." Melissa then walked over to the veils. "I don't think you need these." "Thank you, Lord, for small favors," Andrea said.

Melissa laughed, then pulled out a tiara. "But you will be wearing this."

The tiara was silver and gold twines embedded with teardrop cubic zirconia that looked like diamonds. It sparkled and glinted in the dim-lit office space.

Andrea held her hand out, awaiting the tiara. She turned it this way and that way, watching the light reflect. "It is beautiful. How do you think I should wear my hair with it?"

"I'm not a pro at hair and makeup, but I did hire your stylist to come and do a trial run. She should be here any minute."

Melissa went to the dress rack, moving hanger after hanger of different shrugs and capes to go over Andrea's sleeveless gown. She periodically held one up to the dress on the rack.

"Have you and Jake made up? Your dad told me about the huge misunderstanding."

Caught off guard by Andrea's question, she fumbled with the shrug she was currently looking at, accidentally pulled it off the hanger and tried to reattach it. "Oh, well, I uh—"

Andrea hurriedly added, "You don't have to confide in me. I didn't mean to overstep."

"Oh Andrea, you didn't. Please don't misunderstand. I—" Melissa flopped into a chair. "Actually, I could use a mom to talk to right now."

Andrea's eyes misted and she sat beside Melissa and grabbed her hand. "I will be more than happy to be that figure if you'd like. I know you are a grown woman and independent, but I never had kids and would love to build a relationship with you if you will allow."

Melissa squeezed Andrea's hand. "Thank you. I made a mess of everything. It started back in high school…"

Melissa spilled everything to Andrea, including all the things she kept from her mom and dad in the past. It was as if a dam had been breached and finally everything was able to come out. She sat back in her chair.

"I don't expect him to trust me, but I would love to stay friends with him even though I know deep inside I am in love with him. Being with Jake is so easy when we are together. It always has been."

"That is definitely a lot to take in. Have you discussed any of this with Jake? Does he know how you feel?"

"I believe he understands how I felt in the past but none of my new feelings. As you heard, I screwed up my first date and then there was this morning with Paul and, for some reason, not having the nerve to make sure he knew we were done. But that all ended up working out well. I know he's attracted to Blair, but I don't think he quite knows what to do with actually physically liking someone for a change."

"That is good news, and I also take it that Jake is still meeting you at the gingerbread contest tonight. Hopefully, he will give you the chance to explain."

"I hope I will be able to have him to myself for a while to explain, but I'm not sure how much time we will have with his niece and Susan coming."

Andrea's eyes lit up. "Do you want me to call Susan and get a feel for Jake's mood or feelings? Even though she is no longer my assistant, we are still dear friends."

Melissa thought about it for a few minutes. "However tempting that sounds, I think I am better off not having any more outside influence."

"Hello ladies, I finally made it. Thought I'd never get here with all of the traffic in town." The stylist had arrived, putting an end to Melissa and Andrea's discussion.

Melissa and Andrea both stood.

Melissa turned to Andrea, giving her the warmest hug she had ever given her to date. "Thank you so much, and I am looking forward to you being my new mom."

"Seriously, you are going to make me cry."

"At least you don't have your makeup done, and this way it won't happen tomorrow on your big day. I love you, Andrea, and I am really glad my dad found you."

Andrea hugged her tight. Her warm tears leaked onto the side of Melissa's cheek. "I love you too, Melissa. Thank you." When she pulled back, she pulled a tissue out of her trouser pocket and wiped her eyes. "I've been rather emotional on and off all day. Must be the pre-wedding nerves."

Melissa clapped her hands together. "Let's get this show on the road and see what type of hairstyle works best."

The rest of the day went without a hitch. Melissa's nerves were jittery as she and Jenna walked into Main Street Java. She scanned the cafe for Jake, but he hadn't arrived yet. But what she noticed was the transformation of the cafe into one of the best gingerbread contest sites ever.

The entire place had been transformed. Tables were set up into twenty different stations for contest participants. Each one was ready to go with icing and stacks of a variety of gingerbread shapes. Walter had told Melissa he had a surprise for her and all her hard work around town. He told her she wouldn't be let down, and boy was he right.

Walter had gotten the art department at the high school to help him paint roll-away walls to resemble the inside of a gingerbread house. Beside each painted wall was a photo of the student who did it and a little bio about them. What a way to support the new up-and-coming artist and also make this event even more special.

He took her idea for the selfie stations and had the students go crazy. They were better than she could have imagined. There were at least ten she counted so far set up throughout the cafe for the influencers and locals to pose.

Melissa elbowed Jenna. "Let's go stand in line. I want to put you in the oven." There was the giant oven, like in *Hansel and Gretel*, where someone could go behind the oven door and reenact being saved. There was already a line, and in front of each picture, there was a hashtag list for people to use when posting.

"Oh my gosh, that is too funny." She and Jenna started heading over to the oven when Jake walked in. It was as if the entire room stopped, and the noise faded to silence. Their eyes caught, and he gave her a slight wave, and all of the noise in the room ignited once more.

"Go to him. This can wait." Jenna's words broke Melissa from her trance.

All Melissa could do was nod. She started walking toward Jake. When their eyes met, he began walking toward her, moving his body in and out of the crowd, which seemed to expand, making it harder for them to reach one another.

"You came." Melissa breathed out when they were in front of one another.

"I did."

Someone bumped into Melissa, pushing her into Jake's arms. His hands caught her upper arms, and she looked up at him. The bumper's apology drifted away like an afterthought, but she didn't even care. That one bump was like fate bringing her closer to Jake. Jake and Melissa had no words, but Jake's head came down. Melissa's heart hammered in her chest as she placed her hands on his waist and stood on her tiptoes to bring her face and lips closer to his.

His head tilted down further. He was going to kiss her. Relief, excitement, desire all swirled inside of her. She closed her eyes, waiting.

"Uncle Jake, what are you doing?"

Melissa opened her eyes and lowered her heels. Standing beside them was Jake's niece, watching them both. Melissa turned to Jake and watched him shake his head slightly. She wondered if he, too, was caught in a trance. The moment did almost feel too surreal.

"Hey, Megs, this is Lissy. She is the one I've been talking about this past week."

Megan hugged Melissa at the waist. "I am so happy to meet you. I was sad you didn't come ice skating with us, but Uncle Jake promised you would make a gingerbread house with us. He told me y'all's was the best and your last contest was a night to remember." Megan squeezed her little hands together at her cheek, twisting her body from side to side all dreamy. "Isn't that right, Uncle Jake?"

Melissa smiled. "A night to remember, huh?" That was the night she and Jake were banned from the contest.

She wouldn't forget that night either. They had basically painted their whole bodies in icing and were ordered out of the contest. They stood outside the building, laughing hysterically.

That night, she had just made Jake's hair stand up in white and green icing spikes when Jake had leaned in close. His hand brushed her cheek, and his thumb wiped some icing off of her bottom lip, then he licked his finger. She froze, wanting so badly for him to kiss her but scared that it would ruin their friendship. She did what she did best. She ran off, saying she had to go home.

After hearing Megan's comment, Melissa wondered if Jake had feelings for her back then too.

"Well, it's nice to finally meet you, Megan, and I am truly sorry for not being able to make the ice-skating date. We will have to go another time. Would you like that?"

Nodding her head vigorously, she grabbed Melissa's hand. "Yes. Can we go to the big rink?"

"Megan, don't you dare go making plans again without my approval, young lady." Susan placed her hands on Megan's shoulders, and Megan turned to her mom.

"Awe, momma, please. I want to go ice skating with Melissa. Uncle Jake said she does twirls and looks like a princess on ice. I want to look like that too."

Melissa's heart warmed. She sidled up to Jake. "So, I look like a princess, huh?"

"Well—"

"Hey Melissa, it's good to see you again. You have done an amazing job with everything."

Melissa turned to Jake, who smiled at his sister. Saved by Susan.

"Thank you, but I'm trying to keep it on the down-low. There are a few people here that I don't want to know that I'm working again."

Susan hushed her voice. "I'm so sorry, I didn't know."

"No worries. It's just—"

Jake grabbed her hand. "Sue doesn't need an explanation. Let's go pick out a good table." He turned to Susan and Megan. "Girls, after you've taken a few pictures, come to find us."

Jake pulled Melissa to the other side of the cafe where the tables were set up. She passed by Cheryl and waved as she and Jake found a semi-quiet spot. "We need to talk, and I know that this isn't the best of places. But I need to know what is really going on with you and Paul. I see one thing and hear another. It's confusing."

Melissa grabbed Jake's hands. "I am one hundred percent not with Paul and haven't been for over a year. Technically we were together for six years but never were we committed. We were just together because it was easy. I am available, and I really would like to not be anymore." She took a deep breath. "Jake, I don't think I ever fell out of love with you, and this week has been like a dream come true. I—"

Jake didn't let her finish and pulled her into his arms in a hug.

Just as he was about to kiss her, a little body slammed into their legs, hugging them both.

"Group hug," Megan said.

Melissa wanted to groan, and if she heard right, Jake did. Megan once more prevented her long-awaited kiss, but it didn't matter. Jake forgave her, and as he let her go, he reached for her hand and didn't let go.

"Is it time?" Megan bounced around them and started picking up and inspecting the icing supplies on the table, and popped a gumdrop in her mouth. "I want to start decorating," she said with a mouth full of candy.

"Megan, what have I told you about talking with your mouth full?" Susan admonished and swatted Megan's hand away from reaching for another piece.

Jake let go of Melissa's hand, squatted down to Megan's level, and whispered loudly to her. "If you eat it all, we won't have anything to decorate the houses with, and we need as much as we can so we can win."

S usan, Megan, Melissa, and Jake all had a perfect groove going, getting the Santa's workshop gingerbread house done. They were down to the last fifteen minutes before the timer went off. Melissa had just finished instructing Megan to write "Santa's" on a small piece of gingerbread that they were using for a sign.

Megan tried to hand the tube to Melissa. "I'm done, your turn."

Melissa was finishing up designing the wreath above the door."You can put it on the table. I'm almost done. Why don't you help your mom and Uncle Jake?"

When Melissa was done, she picked up the tube that was squeezed and flopping in the middle. She adjusted the icing, squeezing the tube, but nothing came out. The tip was clogged or possibly bent.

Megan started squirming next to Melissa. "What's wrong, Lissy?"

Melissa couldn't help but smile each time Megan used the nickname Jake made up years ago. "The tip looks to be bent a little, and the icing is stuck."

Megan's eyes teared up. "I'm sorry."

Melissa turned to Megan. "You didn't do anything wrong, honey, don't cry. I can use another tip to write 'workshop' out."

Jake overheard. He handed Susan, who was across the table, the last of the gumdrops to place around the sidewalk leading up to the workshop. Melissa caught Jake and Susan talking to one another silently with only their eyes and a few headshakes. He squatted down to Megan's level. "What do you think you did, Megs?"

She wiped her eyes. "I wanted to taste the icing, and I bit the tip when too much came out."

Whispering loudly he said, "I tasted it too. Maybe I'm the one who broke it."

Megan sniffled. "Can you fix it?"

Jake turned to Melissa, and before he said anything, she handed him the tube with a huge grin. Her heart melted into a puddle of chocolate gooeyness at the way he handled Megan.

"Sue, do you have a safety pin?"

"You know I do." She pulled her purse out from under the table, pulled out a tiny sewing kit, and handed the safety pin to Jake.

Jake shimmied the pin in the tiny hole. "I think I got it." He squeezed the tube and nothing came out. He winked at Megan. "Second time's the charm." He shimmied the pin in again. After pulling the pin out, he used more strength than last time and squeezed the tube hard. The metal tip shot off and the entire tube of icing splattered all over Jake's face.

All three girls gasped. Susan and Melissa laughed, but poor little Megan was in hysterics. "Uncle Jake, you have to hurry and go wash your face." She tried turning him around and shoving him from behind.

"Megan, what has gotten into you?" Susan came around the table in an attempt to try and console her child.

"I don't want to lose. I don't want them to think I started an icing fight and get kicked out." She started shoving him toward the restroom again.

Melissa covered her mouth, trying to hide her laugh.

Susan handed Jake a napkin. "Wipe some of that off your face on your way to the men's room."

"Thanks, Mommy," Megan said as she grabbed one of Jake's hands and started to pull him forward.

Melissa and Susan heard Jake saying, "I've got this, Megs. Go back and help finish the gingerbread house."

Megan looked torn, turning from her uncle whose face was splattered red with icing, and the table where both Melissa and Susan were trying hard not to burst out laughing.

Susan turned to Melissa and handed her a different color icing with a small tip. "I'll say, you and Jake do know how to make a memorable time."

"Thanks." She took the tube and chuckled again. "I guess

we do, don't we?" She finished writing "workshop" as Megan stood by her side, watching her.

Melissa turned to Megan. "Do you want to put the last piece of the sign up?"

Megan nodded.

"Be careful that you don't touch the words. They might smush." "Okay."

They all stood back when the sign was on. Susan stood with her arms crossed, examining their work. "That's a job well done. High five." After she and Megan high-fived, she held her hand up to Melissa.

For the first time in ages, her life seemed to be heading exactly where she always wanted to go. Although she retired early from event planning, she got her groove back, and it was all thanks to Jake. He was a lot like her mom, pointing out the subtle things she did and giving her praises. She never knew that she was the type of person to need affirmations from her loved ones, but somehow it made her more creative.

Maybe her mom was right. Lasting love was worth finding. Melissa started to understand what her mom talked about now that she found the man to fill that role.

He would be there for her in good or bad times. He'd be her encourager, her protector, and even tolerate her when her attitude sucked, or when she screwed up like she did with not knowing how to handle Paul. Her special person would be willing to forgive and stand by her side always. That was lasting love.

She never had that with Paul. Could Jake be her lasting love? Excitement-induced chills raced up her arms and spine at that thought. It sure had been easy picking up where they left off nearly ten years ago, and even though she made him question her honesty about Paul, he forgave her and was willing to let it go. Her heart fluttered in her chest as a wave of happiness overflowed from her.

Scanning the room, joy seemed to fill all her friends and acquaintances in town. Even the influencers laughed and joked as they hurried to finish their gingerbread houses. Walter placed a huge timer on the wall behind the cash register where his menu hung. Only a few minutes left. Her grin spread wider when she spotted a few others besides Jake who had icing all over their faces.

Everyone seemed to be having a really good time. She could almost hear her mom saying, "See, a little fun goes a long way to making any event a success."

Tomorrow night would be the finale, and she couldn't wait to read what the influencers posted when they discovered they would all be attending a wedding.

She was filled with excitement over her and Jake's near kiss, remembering her mom without tears for the first time in two years, and the success of the evening. She wanted Jake by her side to share her happiness. She turned to Susan. "I'm going to go see what's taking Jake so long."

"Y'all hurry back. There are only five more minutes until judging begins."

Melissa rushed to the other side of the cafe toward the restrooms but didn't have to go that far. Jake was near the hallway leading to the back. It was fairly quiet where he was. He was on the phone, his back turned to her. She stepped back to give him some space when his words prevented her from moving any further.

"Yes, she rewrote the whole thing. I am editing it right now." He paused.

Was he talking about her book? Melissa knew she should step away, but now her curiosity was piqued. They had never had the opportunity to talk about her book because of being so busy with the festival and wedding and her big goof-up with Paul. Now she couldn't wait to pick his brains about what he thought of her book.

"Yes Gwendolyn, I understand. And Ben, I don't know how many times I can reiterate this, but I will do everything I can to close the deal, even pretend to be nice. I know you both think I can't act, but I promise you, she will be falling at my feet begging for this proposal."

Melissa stood there in shock. How could he do this to her? She backed away, knocking into a planter.

Jake turned around and had the gall to smile at her. She took off, trying her best not to cry in front of the entire town. Jake reached her and grabbed her arm. "Lissy, wait up."

She stopped and turned around. Tears escaped. Her jaw clenched tight. She slapped him across the face. "Never, and I mean never call me Lissy again. How could you use me and sell me like that? I will never accept any proposal you try to give me."

She stormed out to the crowd around them murmuring and Jake calling her name.

CHAPTER TWENTY-FOUR

Jake started after Melissa, but Megan ran up to him.

"Uncle Jake, hurry, the judging is about to start."

"Megs, I have to go after Lissy."

"You can go later. You promised me we'd try and win."

Jake was conflicted. He needed to go to Melissa, but Megan was little. She wouldn't understand why he was abandoning her. He grabbed her hand and went back to the table.

He hurriedly sent Melissa a text. When he lifted his head, Susan was watching him.

"Where is Melissa? Why is your cheek red, and why do you look like you lost the love of your life all over again? What is going on?"

"She took off. I think she overheard part of my phone call and misunderstood."

Before Jake could explain further, Jenna was standing with the judges in front of their table. Jenna leaned over and, in a whisper, said, "What do you mean she misunderstood your phone call?"

"I was on the phone with work. They had an emergency conference call. I gave them the news a few days back that I wasn't coming back after my sabbatical. We had an issue with one of our long-time authors. This woman only wants me to edit, and they told me that I needed to talk her into signing a new proposal to contract me for the editing but still using the publishing company and their literary agents. I have to go back tomorrow to talk her into it, and I think Melissa must have heard some of it."

Jenna sighed. "This is all insane. First her, now you. What is wrong with you two? When I find Mr. Right, it will not be this challenging. I can promise you that."

The guest judges gave Jenna a look to say "We are done evaluating. Can we move on?" Jenna pulled out her clipboard, also pretending to look at it and jot down notes. She turned to the judges. "We can move on now."

Then she turned to Jake. "One question. Do you want to be with Melissa?"

"Yes. More than anything."

"Then you need to fix this. Find Mel." She took off after the other judges.

The rest of the judging went by slower than maple syrup flowing out of a tree.

He had tried calling Melissa twice, going to voicemail. He left a short message of "we need to talk" both times.

He had to explain in person. He had no idea what part of his conversation she overheard, but when he retraced the conversation in his head, his stomach churned. He could understand why she might have thought it was about her. He hadn't gotten to tell her yet about the agreement he was trying to work out with Ben. He was going to surprise her with all of his news about moving home and freelancing for his company after the wedding.

He sent her several text messages stating practically the same thing.

She ignored them all.

The judges started coming around with the awards and ribbons, and Megan was jumping for joy when they actually came in third place.

Susan held Megan's hand as they were all walking out. "Any word yet?"

"Nothing. After I drop you off, I'm going to go to her house."

"I hope y'all get to talk. It seems it's been nothing but one misunderstanding or another with both of you."

"I do too."

Jake arrived at Melissa's house a few minutes after dropping Susan and Megan off. The lights were all out. He knocked on the door and rang the bell. No answer. His stomach churned. He drove around town looking at all the typical places he knew Melissa went but couldn't find her car anywhere.

He parked in the ice rink parking lot and sent her another message.

The second he put his phone down, it rang. He answered before the caller ID showed.

"Lissy."

His hopes dashed away when his boss's voice boomed over the receiver.

Jake tried to cover up his annoyance as he thrummed his fingers aggressively on the steering wheel. "Hey Ben, what's going on now?"

"Sorry, man, but I just got off the phone with Janet. If we are going to make this work, I need you in the office at seven tomorrow morning. She agreed to meet before her flight. She is heading out to visit her family for the holidays."

Jake was ready to be done with this project and start his new life in Cypressville. "I'll be there. I will make her understand what we decided. I believe she will be happy with the compromise."

Ben hesitated and then blew out a breath. "I do too, but I can assure you we will miss your communication skills with the clients."

Jake turned the car on and headed back home.

When he entered the house, Susan was at the kitchen table drinking a cup of tea. "Did you find her?"

"No. I searched every place I could think of. Now I have to pack and head back to the city. I have a meeting at seven AM."

"Tomorrow's the Christmas tree lighting and the wedding.

You can't miss it."

"I should be back by midday. Janet has only an hour to spare. She has a flight to catch in the morning."

Jake pushed away from the table, walked over to the coffee pot that finished percolating, and started pouring some into a thermos. "If you run into Lissy, can you please tell her this was all a misunderstanding, and I will explain everything to her tomorrow?"

"Of course, I will."

"I realized one thing tonight," he said.

When Jake didn't come out with his thought right away, Susan fidgeted with a few packs of sugar on the table, trying to be patient. After a few silent moments, she finally asked, "What?"

"I don't want to live another moment without her in my

life. I'm not that shy high school boy anymore. This time, I will tell her the truth upfront and wait for her as long as I need to."

Susan got up and walked over to Jake. He stood, and Susan gave him a big hug with tears in her eyes. "I really hope things work out for you. Melissa is a smart woman." She stepped back. "Maybe a little..." she held her forefinger and thumb about an inch apart, "...dramatic in her emotions. But a brilliant girl. She will come round, and this will all work out. You'll see."

Jake gave Susan a half-smile. "I'm going to pack an overnight bag and head home. I will probably give my realtor a call tomorrow while in town to put my apartment on the market. Do you mind if I stay here until I sell and find a place in town?"

"You better! I know Megan will be thrilled to have you here permanently."

"I'll be happy to see her every day too."

"I'm heading to bed. Tomorrow, I need to be at the shop early to unload a few more boxes. Can you believe they bought almost all the mistletoe balls I made?"

"Wow, that's fantastic! Good thing you made so many. I'll stop by there tonight before heading out of town and pull the box down. If I'm not mistaken, it's on one of the higher shelves because they were lightweight. I don't want you climbing and reinjuring your ankle."

"I appreciate that. Pull one out for you. You never know when you'll need one." She winked at him as she turned to climb the stairs. "Oh, and text me when you get home to let me know you made it there safe."

Jake yawned. He went upstairs, packed, grabbed his coffee and headed out of town. He took Susan's advice and grabbed a mistletoe ball out of the box, put it on the front seat next to his bag, and headed home.

The drive back to the city gave Jake clarity in several areas of his life. He was ready to take the plunge and move to Cypressville. After he got Janet on board with his alternative plan, he would still do contract work with Ben and his publishing company and be free to take on his own projects on the side.

That new life meant big changes, and there was one change he was ready for, even if he wasn't sure how it would pan out.

Now more than anything, if he was going to get it, he had to do something so outrageous Lissy would have to believe him. It was imperative she believed he was ready for a relationship with her.

An idea popped into his head. It was completely out of his character, but if he went through with it and it worked... He smiled as his heart fluttered in his chest with the possibilities.

Making a mental list of what he needed to do after his meeting, he knew it would keep him in the city longer than expected. He couldn't wait for the sun to come up so he could get his plans rolling. He laughed out loud and slapped the steering wheel with his hand. His spirits lifted.

"It just might work."

He drove the last hour of his journey finishing his coffee and singing Christmas carols along with the radio.

CHAPTER TWENTY-FIVE

The next morning Melissa woke up to Snickerdoodle licking her hand and whimpering. She had driven around almost all night. Too exhausted to continue home, she pulled over into the parking lot of a large shopping center in Pineville and fell asleep.

Melissa put the leash on Snickerdoodle and brought her to a small patch of grass near the edge of the parking lot to do her business. After walking around for a few minutes, they headed back to the car.

Her phone battery died after sending a text to her dad last night telling him not to worry about her not coming home. She told him she was staying the night at Jenna's. She ignored all of Jake's calls and messages last night but in the light of day this morning she reevaluated the situation.

Back in the car, she plugged her phone back in, and once it came on, she had over seventy messages from Jake. She rubbed her face hard and groaned out loud. "What have I done?"

She turned to the rearview mirror and glared at her eyes.

"You silly, silly girl. Why do you always run away when you're afraid?"

She turned her attention back to the phone. "Time to face the music." She started scrolling through her messages. Jake sent so many messages saying to please call him. The most recent said, "If you don't call me, I will be on stage at the tree lighting waiting for you. You won't be able to run away from me there. You'll have to listen to me. It's important."

She held the phone to her chest and breathed out a long sigh. Jake shouting that she misunderstood kept playing on repeat this morning, but last night, her emotions were all over the place, and she didn't want to listen to him.

Her slapping him and running away was a repeat of high school, and she wanted to cry at the absurdity of her actions. She was a grown woman. Why did she have to revert to her childish ways when she had finally understood her feelings for Jake? She loved him and wanted to be with him, but rather than listening to him, she let the phone call incident become another Molly.

If she hadn't been afraid in the past, Jake may never have married Molly. There is a significant possibility that she and Jake would have been the ones married instead. But she ruined it back then, and she ruined it again this time. What good did opening her heart do if she followed in her past self's footprints?

But what if she had understood his phone call? Did she really know Jake? Ten years is a long time. People can change. And is a week too quick to rediscover someone?

Melissa rubbed her aching heart. The grief of possibly losing Jake was nearly as painful as when she lost her mom. How could this have happened so fast? She wanted to believe in the lasting love her mom spoke of, but to discover that Jake used her for her book, if it were true, that would shatter her spirit more than the governor's ball and all the horrible media last year.

She didn't know if she could bounce back this time.

Was Jake trying to cover up the truth by telling her she misunderstood? Was it all a scheme to move him up the corporate ladder, she could never trust him again. That to her was worse than having her name dragged through the mud.

They might accept her book this time around, but this time she was the one rejected, by Jake.

There is no mistake in rejection. It's a done deal.

Her dad's ringtone, "Carol of the Bells," chimed out from her phone. She answered over the car's Bluetooth. "Hey, Dad."

"Andrea doesn't want to see me today. Bad luck to see the bride on the wedding day. But I forgot my tux in her office yesterday when I went to pick her up for lunch. She'll be there most of the day getting ready. Do you think you can swing by and pick it up for me before coming home to change?"

"Sure, I'm on my way there now. It may be about an hour or two before I get it to you at home. I have a few things to tie up as well. Will that be all right?"

"Technically, I don't need it until six, so take your time. I just wanted to make sure you have it before Andrea locks up her office."

"No problem, talk to you later, Dad. Love you."

"Love you too, Sugarplum." Funny how just weeks ago, when her dad used to call her that, it always seemed like he had something bad to tell her. Now it felt for the first time like a true endearment.

Melissa pressed the call button on her steering wheel. "Call Jenna."

Jenna's phone rang several times before voicemail picked up. "Start the gossip now."

Melissa usually got a kick out of Jenna's message, but today not so much. "Hey, sorry I didn't call back last night. I'm sure you probably heard all the gossip about what happened last night already so I won't go into detail on this message. Sorry if I worried you by not answering your calls last night, and if anyone asks, tell them I slept at your house. I ended up driving around most of the night thinking. I can't believe I made another scene with Jake. I swear I think you were right when you said love should be easy and this isn't. Half the town plus all the influencers probably caught it on film. I am so embarrassed and stressed that I ruined the town's charm we were all aiming for. My phone is on now, so please call me. I need your advice. I don't know what to do."

The tears started again, and she sniffled. "Before I overheard him, he nearly kissed me twice. I literally, within moments, had visions of him and I getting married one day. I can't believe I fell for him again and so fast. Call me when you get this and be prepared because once tonight is over, I'll need a girls' night with a good cry and lots of ice cream, and..." The message tone beeped, indicating the time ran out.

She had her finger hovering over the call button to call back and finish her message, but in the end, she didn't. She was only rambling anyway and would probably have to repeat everything to Jenna in person when she saw her next. At least she would know what happened and hopefully not judge her too harshly.

She made her way back into town. She had a lot of loose ends to tie up before tonight, and the annoying little voice in the back of her mind told her not to plan on Jake helping. He probably wouldn't be in town, anyway.

As she parked her car at City Hall, she exhaled, wiped her eyes once more, and whispered, "Good riddance."

Snickerdoodle barked at her. "I know. I don't really mean it, but if I don't try and harden my heart, I won't make it through the day or—" she choked out the last words, "Dad's wedding."

Melissa rubbed Snickerdoodle in her favorite spot behind her ear. When her little paw started thumping on the seat of the car, Melissa's tears finally subsided. "If only people could love as unconditionally as you, life would be so much easier."

CHAPTER TWENTY-SIX

*E*ntering the near-empty building, Melissa hurried to Andrea's office to pick up her dad's tux. The door was slightly ajar. Melissa knocked softly three times.

"Come in," Andrea chimed.

Melissa opened the door to Andrea sitting behind her desk. Her office was still littered with a large, portable three-way mirror and circular stand, hanging racks with her dress, shawl, and tiara. The makeup and hair station were fully loaded with all the supplies needed to turn Andrea into a beautiful Christmas bride.

Andrea stood up and walked over to Melissa, hugging her, then giving Snickerdoodle a head rub. "Thank you for picking up your dad's tux."

Melissa placed the dog on the floor and scanned the room for her dad's tux.

"No problem." Anxiety over last night blossomed in her chest. Before Andrea got up to receive her she could have sworn she gave her a look of sympathy and disappointment before a smile reached her lips.

"Andrea, I..." Before she got the words out, unwilling

tears flowed, and before long, Andrea became the mother she had lost and wrapped her in an embrace. She rubbed her back in small circles the same way her mom used to, and it made her cry all the harder.

When the tears finally subsided, Melissa pulled back, wiping her eyes on the cuff of her jacket. "I am so sorry. I feel like I have ruined everything, the whole festival is ruined because of me, and I'm so worried tonight will be even worse because I'll be there."

Melissa started crying again, and Andrea pulled her in for another hug. Exhaling deeply into Andrea's shoulder, she said, "Today's supposed to be your day, and here I am, being selfish, crying on your shoulder."

"I don't mind. Honestly, I don't know what to do with myself today. The only thing on my agenda is tree lighting and my wedding tonight."

Andrea moved her hands to Melissa's shoulders and pushed her back slightly, looking her in the eyes. "You have done nothing wrong and have only made my life and my special day more beautiful and meaningful than Elise would have. I can guarantee it." She grabbed a tissue and dabbed it under Melissa's eyes. "Can you tell me what all these tears are about?"

"Do you really believe everything is okay after last night?"

"What do you mean last night? What happened?"

"You and Dad were at the gingerbread contest. Didn't everyone talk about the big spectacle your future daughter was going to be?"

Andrea pulled Melissa by the hand and led her to the two chairs that used to be in front of her desk, now pushed off to the side of the office behind the hanging rack.

"Sit down and tell me where all this is coming from in detail because I am very lost."

Melissa explained everything going on with Jake, and

exactly what she overheard on the phone, and what she did to Jake.

After she finished explaining, she waited with bated breath for what Andrea would do or say. Andrea didn't say anything, only pulled out her phone and opened up the app where the influencers had been posting all about Cypressville's Winter Festival.

She turned her phone to Melissa. "Look, nothing but fun photos documenting a wonderful time."

Andrea was right, as Melissa could see as she scrolled through nearly all the accounts. Each one contained silly moments. Even Blair and Paul laughing with icing on each of their noses, holding up a barely standing gingerbread house. Melissa handed the phone back to Andrea.

"Wow, I thought my slapping Jake in front of everyone would be plastered all over the sites by now. I can honestly say I'm surprised."

"Melissa, honey, I hope you don't mind me butting my nose into your business, but as we are soon to be family, I will impart some wisdom to you. You need to stop worrying about what everyone thinks and live your life. You completely shut down last year after one bad review with extenuating circumstances that were completely out of your control. When that happens, you need to keep your head up and show everyone you are stronger than the ones trying to sabotage you. And you and Jake, if you ask me..." Andrea gave Melissa a pointed stare.

Melissa urged her on with a lift of her chin.

"I think you misunderstood the phone call and are getting yourself all worked up over nothing. You obviously over-heard something that may have sounded like you, but you don't have all the details to make an informed decision. For all you know, he could've been speaking of another client. I am sure Jake has more than one female novelist he edits for.

Possibly, that was who he was speaking about. Let me ask you a question. Have you signed any contracts with Jake? Because if you didn't, you aren't his client. Why would he be talking to his boss about you?"

Melissa shook her head as she sat there in shock. That thought had never crossed her mind. Digging deep within herself, she discovered the horrible truth. She was afraid she wasn't worthy of Jake and could never compare to Molly. She made too many mistakes with him and it was easier to run when the chance presented itself.

When she looked up at Andrea, their eyes connected. "I made a terrible mistake. Oh, Andrea, how will I ever make this one up to him? A phone call won't do. He said he'd be at the gazebo waiting for me tonight, but after I ignored his calls all day, I'm not sure if he will be there after what I did."

"Well, if you want my advice." Before the words left Andrea's mouth Melissa was already nodding.

"Yes, tell me what to do."

"After the wedding, stop running and go after that boy then never let him out of your grip again. He's a good one."

Snickerdoodle woke up just at that moment and barked happily, running to Andrea as if she too was in agreement. Both women laughed as Andrea picked up Snickerdoodle.

The rest of the day went by in a flurry of activity. Melissa and Jenna kept missing each other's calls. The caterer arrived and was preparing the atrium for after the ceremony. She had just met Mr. McFarlan and told him where to park the carriage out of sight from the passersby.

Everything was all ready for the tree lighting and ceremony, which were due to take place very soon.

She went into Andrea's office. "Are you ready?"

"Absolutely."

"I have the carriage parked just outside the back door. At exactly six PM, you will need to be in the carriage and heading down Main Street. Dad and I will wait at the gazebo." Melissa gave Andrea a gentle hug and kissed her cheek. "Welcome to the family."

"Do not make me cry, young lady. This makeup took forever to apply."

Melissa turned to walk out and turned back around. "See you soon, Mom." She winked and hurried out of the office before Andrea could say another word.

Laughing to herself as she went down the hall, she double-checked that Cheryl had everything under control.

"How's everything here? Almost ready?"

"Yes. And Melissa, thanks again for the help with the flowers, with the low lighting, and all the things you made me buy that actually turned out stunning. I would never have been able to do this without your help."

"It really was a no-brainer once we got started. Make sure that Chef François has the hors d'oeuvres ready and the servers prepared with champagne at seven for the crowd to make their way here."

"Will do." Cheryl made a note on her clipboard. "See you later."

Melissa went into the restroom to touch up her makeup and change into her dress. During the day when she went into Walter's, he had detained her for a few minutes. Jenna had left a dress bag with him, telling him how they kept missing each other, and she found the perfect dress out of her closet for Melissa.

Jenna had often tried to dress Melissa up in way more

flamboyant dresses than she would normally wear. The black dress was the exception, but that, too, being so form-fitting, was still normally out of her comfort zone. So, with all intentions of wearing the dress she picked out and was about to put on, she decided, what the heck? Why not look at what Jenna picked?

The dress was stunning. It was a vintage dark green velvet and looked almost identical to Rosemary Clooney's dress in *White Christmas*. She hurriedly put her pantyhose on, then the dress, and decided on a bright red lipstick. Her hair hung in waves around her shoulder, and even though her life wasn't settled in all the ways she'd like, she was excited about Christmas.

She was humming as she walked down the street. When she spotted her dad standing in the gazebo, she made her way to meet him. With shining eyes, her dad held his hand out to her to help her up the steps in her heels. "Sugarplum, you look just like your mom."

She hugged him. "I do?"

He pushed back, held her at the shoulders. "Spitting image."

"I think Mom would be really happy to hear that and very pleased with your choice in Andrea." She tilted her head slightly. "Now that I think about it, I wonder if Mom encouraged you to get involved with local politics in her last year because she was trying all along to set you up with Andrea."

"You aren't too far off. Andrea confided in me not too long ago that she and your mother had quite the conversation before she was too sick to leave the house. You know your mother and how involved she was with everything. She encouraged Andrea to run for office. She had already put a kind word about Andrea all over town, giving her stamp of approval. And Mom also told her that if she wasn't alive to see it, she insisted she enlist me to help her win. I think your mom picked Andrea for me and me for Andrea. She knew we would need each other and fall in love."

Melissa hugged her dad. "Mom was exceptional. I will always miss her, but I think she picked Andrea for me too."

Her dad pulled out his handkerchief and handed it to Melissa.

"Wipe those eyes. We don't want your mascara to run." Melissa laughed. "When did you finally learn the lingo?"

"I've watched enough movies to know that women don't like raccoon eyes."

Melissa pressed the handkerchief under her eyes. "How's it look?"

"Perfect."

"Good." She held a dry part of the handkerchief to his eyes and patted away his residual tears. The clock chimed six. "You ready?"

"Yes, very."

Melissa walked to the microphone. "Good evening and welcome to Cypressville. I want to start the night off by thanking all of our guests here this evening for attending our first annual Christmas Festival. And to our very special guests, the influencers who have taken time out of their busy schedules to spend a week with us in our hometown."

Melissa scanned the audience and tried to make eye contact with each influencer. "You have all become a part of our small town family and hope you will always consider Cypressville your home away from home. And lastly, thank you to the citizens of Cypressville for coming together and making all of this possible. Without your warmth and sense of community, none of this would have been possible. And without further ado, I give you Mayor Jackson."

There was no movement, and all was silent. Then all the lights went out. The crowd began chattering and looking around. Melissa put her hand over the microphone and turned to her dad, pretending to appear concerned, when a soft violin from far away started playing Pachelbel's Canon in D. The only lights that could be seen were at the far end of Main Street. Everyone was turning this way, wondering what was happening, and searching for the sound.

Soon instrument after instrument joined in, each artist standing a few feet apart on each side of the road. By the time the last musicians began playing, the entire street was glowing with candles lining a path to the gazebo. The entire group of onlookers chattered excitedly, wondering what was happening. The influencers all had their phones out recording.

Finally, the horses pulling the carriage with Andrea could be seen. The carriage was a white Cinderella one, illuminated by gold lanterns with flickering flames within.

They arrived at the gazebo, and the driver wearing a suit hopped down and helped Andrea out of the carriage. Cheryl was there to help smooth out the train of Andrea's gown.

Melissa linked arms with her dad. "Surprise."

Her dad beside her was smiling, eyes glistening once more, not out of sadness but out of pure joy at seeing his bride. "When did you plan this grand entrance? You never once mentioned it to Andrea or me, as I recall, in any of our planning meetings."

"I only told Andrea today about the carriage. It was my gift to you both. I love you very much."

He grabbed her hand and squeezed it tight.

"Now go meet your bride and help her up the steps."

While Frank went down the steps to meet his bride, the Justice of the Peace stood in front of the tree. Melissa stood off to the side, searching for Jake. His message said he'd be here, but he was nowhere to be found. Susan and Megan were right up front, and she caught Susan's eyes briefly. Susan lifted her shoulders and mouthed, "He should be here."

Melissa had a sinking feeling deep inside that Jake wouldn't be there. She ruined everything once more by over-reacting and being too impulsive. That was obviously something that she was really good at and needed to work on changing in the future.

She didn't want to cry about her loss when she needed to be happy for her dad. He helped Andrea up the steps as Cheryl arranged her train beautifully to flow down over the steps. The entire gazebo was decorated in green garland, and candles hung from each section of the octagon giving off a warm glow. It would make a beautiful photo, and she was glad everyone was taking pictures.

Melissa held the microphone to her mouth once more. "Surprise! You are all formally invited to attend the wedding of Mayor Andrea Jackson to Mr. Frank Albright."

The crowd cheered and clapped. Melissa handed the microphone to the Justice of the Peace, which started the ceremony and ended when both her dad and Andrea finished exchanging rings.

"I now pronounce you man and wife. You may now kiss your bride."

Frank placed his hands on Andrea's face and gave her a gentle kiss on her lips as Melissa simultaneously pressed the button, lighting up the Christmas tree illuminating the newly married couple.

The entire group cheered, a smile brightening each face in the crowd. One of the influencers' voices boomed louder than the rest, "Best Christmas festival ever!"

Melissa's heart soared. She did it! Not only did she organize an amazing wedding, but also a series of week-long events that seemed to bring everyone pleasure.

She was back!

She wrapped her arms around her waist, calming the massive swarm of butterflies fluttering inside at the thought of succeeding. She had forgotten how much she loved event planning. Never in a million years after last year's fiasco would she have ever expected to plan another event, but life had a way of forcing you out of your comfort zones.

If only she could make her life with Jake as easy as planning this event.

Once more, she searched the crowd, hoping to spot him. Her grip tightened around her waist as the butterflies dipped and swirled uncomfortably. She took a deep breath, loosened her arms, and walked up to the microphone.

"If I could get everyone's attention. Mr. and Mrs. Albright." She turned her head to Andrea and her dad and graced them with an enormous smile. "Would like to invite each and every one of you to their wedding reception being held in the atrium of City Hall. If you could all make your way there, Chef François has hors d'oeuvres ready."

Melissa walked over to her dad, giving him a hug and a kiss on the cheek. He gave her a firm hug back.

"Thank you, Sugarplum."

She then turned to Andrea, hugging her. Andrea squeezed her tight. "Everything was perfect. A night I will always remember. Thank you."

"You're welcome." Melissa kissed her on the cheek. "Now, let's detach this train so you both can get a ride back to City Hall."

CHAPTER TWENTY-SEVEN

*A*s the photographer was finishing up the private bride and groom photoshoot outside of City Hall, Melissa entered the atrium.

Walter stood near the entrance, waiting. "Are they about done?"

"Yes, they are taking the last of the private photos."

Melissa scanned the venue to make sure everything was going smoothly. François stood behind a long buffet table, directing his staff in preparation for dinner to be served after the first few dances. Hors d'oeuvres were being passed around on silver trays by servers in black suits and gloves. Everything down to the table cloths looked very elegant. Even the centerpieces she and Cheryl had to adjust sparkled under the candlelight.

Andrea and her dad walked up behind her. Melissa turned when she heard Andrea's breath catch. Andrea's smile was enormous. She hugged Melissa. "You've outdone your-self. It's perfect."

Melissa's dad squeezed her hand. "Thank you, Sugarplum."

Melissa smiled back. Her heart thawed out even though her romantic life didn't turn out the way she hoped. Christmas had been horrible the last two years of her life, and this Christmas she discovered family was more than just her mom and dad. Family comprised the people she came to love and care about. She gave Walter the signal, and the band started playing softly.

Walter lifted the microphone. "I am honored to introduce you to Mr. and Mrs. Mayor Albright."

Everyone cheered, few laughed, and someone whistled rather loudly. Melissa laughed when she noticed Jenna spinning her cloth napkin over her head and swiveling her hips. Jenna's dad joined her, laughing, but her mom hid behind her hand, shaking her head at her husband and daughter.

This crazy, fun-loving group of citizens was her extended family, and for the first time in a long time, she was glad she moved home.

The moment Andrea and dad moved onto the dance floor, the singer began singing "At Last" by Etta James. Melissa watched from the edge of the dance floor. The happiness from moments before dipped briefly when a vision of her and Jake dancing flashed inside her brain. She swallowed the hint of jealousy down, focusing hard on her parents glowing in newly wedded bliss.

Several community members came up to her, complimenting her on how beautiful the ceremony was and how surprised they were that the wedding had moved up. After the third time, Melissa explained the reason. The words clicked into place. The sadness in her heart healed this season thanks to Andrea's words. Andrea told her the main reason she wanted to surprise the town was that the community was her family. She was close to each and every person and wanted to share her special day with them all, and a small church wedding in the new year wouldn't allow for all of her family to come. Then once she invited the influencers, that was when it became a surprise.

Melissa stopped in her tracks when she realized she had just had those exact sentiments. Smiling bigger, she headed toward Andrea and her dad finishing their dance. She'll have to thank Andrea for sharing that little piece of wisdom with her.

The next song started up, and her dad and Andrea continued dancing.

A finger tapped her shoulder as a deep voice spoke near her ear. "May I have this dance?"

Melissa swallowed hard. Her heart rate accelerated as she turned to see Jake standing behind her. His hair was messy, like when he ran his hands in it when stressed. His tie was crooked, and his buttons looked as if he skipped one, but he was here. He showed up.

Jake's Adam's apple bobbed up and down from swallowing, but he held his hand out to her. Hope blossomed in her chest and she took a deep breath and placed her hand in his. Jake's body visibly relaxed, and the crease between his brows smoothed. It was as if his body deflated all his anxiety. He stood back straight again and breathed out. "Thank you."

He led Melissa to the floor, and they began dancing. This was their first dance. Since prom all those years ago, she dreamed of this moment. So many things had happened since prom, so many misunderstandings. She did it again last night and knew beyond a doubt she had to apologize. Jake showed up. In all his messages, he told her she misunderstood. She knew in her heart she was wrong and jumped to conclusions, and that no matter what she would always work to have open communications with him in the future.

When half of the song had been sung, they both spoke at the same time.

"Jake"

"Melissa."

"Jake, let me go first."

He nodded.

"I jumped to conclusions, and I shouldn't have. I have a bad habit of when I'm scared that things are going well or I don't want to ruin something that could be great, I sabotage myself. I don't know why I do it other than to protect myself, but in the long run, it doesn't really protect me." She paused, not knowing how else to say what she wanted to say.

He seemed to take her pause as her being done. "That conversation was about one of my clients at the publishing company I used to work for. We were trying to create a new contract where I will still be exclusive to all of my clients for their editing needs and be contracted from my publishing company. My boss, Ben, and I are good friends, and the company is a small publishing house. He has the right to do whatever he wants, and he wants to keep me in any way he can. I'm moving to Cypressville. I want to be with you."

Melissa moved her arms over Jake's shoulders, bringing her body flush to him. His hands tightened on her waist. "I want to be with you too." She breathed out, their faces so close.

Jake's hand moved on her back, pressing her closer into him, and their lips met. Sparks flew behind Melissa's eyes, and a roaring in her ears blared as all the sensations of her first kiss with Jake ignited beyond anything she ever imagined. When they broke apart, the roaring didn't stop.

A small group of their closest friends was near them, clapping. Even Paul and Blair were smiling at them.

Melissa leaned her forehead on Jake's shoulders, blushing profusely. He lifted her head with his hand. "Did I ever tell you how much I love it when you blush?"

She felt her cheeks warm up, and her eyes were glazed over in pure joy. "Have I ever told you how much I love you?"

Her hand instinctively flew over her mouth, clamping it shut. Then she dropped her hand and stuttered out. "I mean, how much I love it when you are all rumpled out of stress. Uh, your buttons are all out of sync." She tried to cover up her embarrassing confession. Just because he was willing to give her a chance to date, she was sure he didn't want to be rushed into a love confession.

He gave her a crooked smile. The one he used when he was up to something. He gazed into her eyes and started unbuttoning his shirt.

"Jake, what are you doing?" She tried to swat at his hands over his buttons. "You can't take your shirt off here."

He laughed as she grabbed his elbow and tugged him away from the dance floor. "I'm not taking my shirt off. I'm fixing my buttons. I was running late and got dressed in the car on my way back into town."

"Oh!"

Done with his buttons he laced his fingers with hers, brought her hand to his lips and kissed it. Then with the same hand lifted their arms and spun her around and started dancing with her again. When she placed her right hand on his waist, Jake pulled her in closer and pressed his cheek gently to hers, whispering into her ear. "I'm sorry I'm late. I was so worried you would deny me a dance because you were mad."

"You don't need to apologize. It was really all my fault."

"No, it wasn't. I should have told you my plans. I should have told you I decided to stay. If I did, you would have never questioned my feelings for you."

Walter was on the mic again. "Ladies and gentlemen, Andrea and Frank would like to say a few words. Please be seated, and dinner will be served right after. Melissa, would you be a dear and come on stage as well?" He handed the microphone to Andrea.

Melissa turned to Jake. "I'll see you soon." She took the liberty of giving him a peck on his cheek before she walked away, heart soaring in happiness.

When she got on stage, Andrea grabbed her hand and said into the mic, "Cypressville, thank you for being my home and my family. When I moved here as a little girl, this town and the people were welcoming to my family. When my parents died when I was a young adult, my friends and the community took me in, and never once did I feel abandoned or alone. Tonight, you all are my family, even our visitors who have so kindly taken a week out of their lives to come to enjoy our festival and tree lighting. They have shared their stories with me, and I now feel connected to them. Frank and I are so honored to call you family. But there is one member of this family that has gone above and beyond to make this week and this night the most magical night of my life."

Andrea unclasped her hand from Melissa's and put her arm around her. "My new daughter, Melissa, last minute took up the mantle as an event planner when Elise, as you all know, snuck off and eloped."

Andrea turned to Elise, who stood off to the side of the stage and winked at her. She had come back that morning and was standing off to the side of the stage, hiding her face in her new husband's shoulder. A few men around him clapped him on his back in congratulations.

"We were so lucky that Melissa agreed to take on the responsibility. She pulled everything together in less than a week. She upgraded every event and pulled the whole community together. A community that had slowly, without knowing it, started drifting apart. This festival saved our town. I am proud and honored to be her second mom."

She handed the mic to Frank and hugged Melissa, and

whispered in her ear. "Thank you. Cheryl just told me that as of this afternoon we are no longer bankrupt. The festival and influencers worked. It's all because of you. You saved our community, and I can never thank you enough."

The whole town was applauding.

The rest of the night passed in a whirlwind.

After the announcement that she was the event planner, person after person came up to her and thanked her for the best festival ever.

Sarah and Alex Holstead let her know they would set up the rink again next Christmas. Mr. Stevens thanked her for encouraging him to host the live-action performance because it helped bring him out of his grief by introducing him to the high school drama club. He told her the school invited him to work with the drama department all year and that next year he would host *A Christmas Carol* again, only this time he'd start planning months ahead.

Paul and Blair came up to her, both giving her accolades. Blair hugged her and took a selfie. "You truly are an amazing event planner. I'm sorry I was so rude to you the first night we met." She glanced at Paul, who held her hand, then back to Melissa. "I misjudged you. Paul was right when he said you were a gem." She kissed Melissa on the cheek and turned away. After a few steps, she turned back around. "I'll be back next year. Follow my blog, you'll have a spotlight, and I promise it will be a rave review."

Melissa watched Blair and Paul leave, happy that they found one another. She searched the last of the crowd for Jake and didn't see him anywhere. Jenna came up to her. "If you're looking for Jake, he took Susan and Megan home. He said he'd be back in a bit. Are you still staying at my place tonight?"

"Yes, if that's all right?"

"Absolutely. The wedding was beautiful. I knew you would pull it off."

"Thanks. I couldn't have done it without everyone's help. This whole thing was a town event, and everyone really came through."

Jenna sat on a chair and took her shoes off, rubbed her feet for a bit, then put them back on. "Too true. If you don't mind, I'm going to head home. These heels are killing me. Remind me

never to wear a new pair of heels to a wedding again."

"I shouldn't be too much longer."

"No worries, you have a key. If I'm asleep, let yourself in." Jenna left.

Walter came up to her and kissed her on the cheek. "Sugar, you sure surprised a lot of folks coming out of that so-called retirement of yours. You going to start your own business in town, now that the cat's outta the bag?"

"Lord, Walter, don't ask me that. I swear that's a thought that never entered my mind. Last year all I could think about was never planning another event again. And you know, secretly, I've always wanted to be a writer."

"I remember you coming into my shop as a kid with that notebook always scribbling. Your momma used to say that your head was full of magical places, and one day you'd write a bestseller."

"She did?" Shocked, Melissa tried to recall her mom's reactions back in high school.

Her mom had always read her stuff with a smile but never encouraged her to take up writing as a career. If she ever mentioned writing as more than a hobby, her mom would always tell her to keep on dreaming. She took those words to mean she wouldn't make it in the real world as a writer and to keep dreaming.

It was the reason she went to college for business with a design minor instead of English and chose event planning. She and her mom would spend hours talking about events she would plan. Had her mother actually meant her to keep dreaming as in to keep writing? She'd have to think about that more.

"Of course, she did. Your momma knew things us average folk didn't understand. She had vision and a loving heart that spread far and wide and will last to eternity."

Melissa smiled, realizing she wasn't sad thinking of her mom. She was happy to hear Walter talk about her. He was right; she had thought the lasting love her mom spoke of was romantic love, but it turned out lasting love was the love you keep in your heart. The love that grows whether a person is here on earth or not. That lasting love is inside each person, ready to be passed on to those around them. She graced Walter with a hug.

"Thank you for telling me this. Do you want to hear a secret?"

"You know I love gossip just as much as Jenna. Of course, I want to hear."

Melissa laughed. "I think my book is going to be published this spring."

Walter hugged Melissa. "Congratulations, sugar."

"But planning... I don't know. I don't think I can choose event planning instead of writing, especially when I have an idea for a sequel."

Jake came up behind her and wrapped his arms around her waist, his head next to hers. "Not to barge in and eavesdrop, but who says you can't do both?"

"Now there's a man with a plan," Walter said, winking at both Melissa and Jake. Jake hugged her tighter as Walter patted Jake on the shoulder and started walking off, saying,

"I'm glad you two both got your heads screwed on straight. I've been saying it since you were kids, you two belong together."

Melissa turned around in Jake's arms. "Together, I like the sound of that."

He leaned down and kissed her.

Christmas Eve arrived. Melissa woke up to Snickerdoodle licking her face. "Good morning, sweet girl." She reached up and petted her on the head. "It's Christmas Eve!" She squealed and wiggled like a child under the covers.

Sitting up in bed, she held Snickerdoodle's face to hers. Her tail wagged happily. "You feel it too, huh girl? This will be the best Christmas in a long time. The whole family is together." Snickerdoodle tilted her head and barked.

"Yep, you heard that right. I have a new lease on life. This Christmas has taught me that my family isn't just Mom and Dad, it is Andrea, Jake and his family, Jenna, and my extended family of Cypressville."

When she put Snickerdoodle down the puppy started circling on her bed. Hurriedly Melissa got up, bringing the puppy to the potty pad she kept in her room for when she didn't wake up fast enough to bring her outside. "Sorry, girl."

Snickerdoodle barked happily when she finished her business and followed Melissa around the room as she started to get ready. Happiness flooded her once more, knowing that when she walked out her bedroom door the house would be full.

Her dad and Andrea came home earlier than expected, only staying away four days instead of their planned two-week honeymoon. But last night they called while she and Jake were ordering at Main Street Java, making it possible for everyone to be together this year. Her Christmas cheer went up three levels when her dad surprised her, letting her know he and Andrea were returning early because they both wanted to spend Christmas together as a family.

Walter, of course, overheard her dad's booming voice from her phone and insisted that he wanted to gift the newlyweds with a celebratory breakfast, and shouted for them to all dress their Christmas best.

Melissa's phone chimed from her nightstand. Dashing to get it, she picked it up and her grin widened after she opened the text. Jake sent a picture of himself with a collared shirt and tie on and a giant bow on his head.

> JAKE: Looking forward to seeing you at breakfast. How do you like your present?

> MELISSA: I love it! But I thought we were saving our gifts until tomorrow morning?

> JAKE: This one is special, though. LOL

> MELISSA: You are special:) See you soon XOXO.

Throwing the phone on her bed, she went back to getting dressed, humming "That Holiday Feeling."

Frank and Andrea were kissing under one of the mistletoe balls she hung up in the doorway into the kitchen. She had hung up the decorations the moment she got home from the reception. She yanked out every piece of mistletoe she could find, placing them around the house as a joke for when Jake came over and he'd have to kiss her. But, seeing her dad and Andrea enjoying it and using it as an excuse to kiss also, made her insides all warm and fuzzy. Love was a remarkable feeling.

"Merry Christmas, lovebirds!"

Her dad stepped away from his new bride, embraced Melissa in a warm hug, and kissed her cheek. "Good morning,

Sugarplum. I see you had fun while we were gone."

He glanced at the mistletoe. Melissa felt her cheeks warm.

Andrea nudged Frank aside. "Stop picking on our girl." She took a few steps toward Melissa and hugged her.

"I'm so glad you are back."

"I am too." Andrea squeezed her tight then released her. "How could we spend our first Christmas as a family away? Frank and I have kept our originally planned honeymoon reservations to go skiing in Colorado at Mardi Gras. This was just a brief trip to get acquainted with being together twenty-four-seven. It was easy to cut it short." She winked at Frank.

"Already sick of him, huh?"

"Hey now!" Frank tweaked Melissa's cheek. "It's Christmas.

You're supposed to be kind and generous of spirit." "True, true." Melissa gave her dad a peck on his cheek.

The alarm on Andrea's watch chimed. "You both ready?" Andrea turned to Melissa after stopping the alarm. "Is Jake meeting us here or Main Street Java?"

"There."

Frank grabbed their coats and handed each one to the ladies, opened the back door leading to the garage, bowed, and swept his hand in the direction of the exit like a true Southern gentleman of long ago. "After you, ladies."

Main Street was crowded with traffic. From the back seat, Melissa glanced around. "We might have to park at City Hall and walk. I'm surprised that so many people are out this morning."

Andrea turned to Frank. Her expression was strained and the line in the center of her brow was enhanced. Her eyes were talking to her dad in a way she never noticed before. Her dad, obviously understanding, lifted his shoulders in answer. She huffed.

Melissa loved the way they interacted. It appeared as if they had been together for ages and knew each other inside and out. After a few more seconds of their silent conversation, she started worrying. Andrea seemed stressed. Did something happen that she wasn't aware of? Was the town having issues with finances again? Did one of the influencers recant their enjoyable time in town? Rather than stress over any more possibly irrational theories, she decided she wasn't the old Melissa anymore and would face whatever horrible thing happened head-on.

Even though that was the case, she still found herself petting Snickerdoodle sleeping on her lap for comfort. "Is everything okay? If something is wrong, I can handle it."

Frank looked in the rearview, and Melissa caught his eyes. "It's fine." His eyes went back to the road as he turned into the parking lot of City Hall in search of a free parking spot.

"Well, that's very forthcoming of you both." She chuffed with a sarcastic laugh.

Andrea turned back in her seat, facing Melissa. "I was hoping it would be empty this early. I was aiming to still take advantage of my honeymoon status until after Christmas. But, with so many people out and about, I hope I don't get bombarded. I didn't mean to make you worry."

Relief washed through Melissa. Then, with a twinge of guilt, feeling a bit self-centered, she automatically assumed the concerns were about her. She patted Andrea on the shoulder and decided then and there to figure out how to prevent a mob if one should occur. "No worries. Dad and I will ward them off if they come to you with anything but congratulations and well wishes."

Andrea gave her dad another look and patted Melissa's hand, still on her shoulder. "Thanks, honey."

They finally found a parking spot and started walking toward Walter's.

Melissa said, "It is strangely busy for a Christmas Eve morning. I wonder what is going on to bring so many people out, but specifically, why are they crowding Main Street Java when Walter promised this would be a simple small break-fast for close friends?"

As they got closer, Melissa could see what drew them in. It was snowing!

Huge, white fluffy fluffy-looking flakes that looked like snow were being pumped from two large machines, turning the entrance to Walter's place into a white Christmas. She had always wanted to come to Main Street Java in the snow; it was a dream she had since she and Jake wrote that silly paper about it back in high school. But living down south, it rarely ever snowed, and technically, it still hadn't. Why did

Walter get a snow machine? The fake snow machine had to have been running for hours; the piles of ice chips were piled so high it had to be inches deep.

Melissa turned to her dad and Andrea. "What in the world is going on?"

"No idea," Frank replied.

Her dad wedged his way in between the crowd. As they broke through, Bing Crosby singing "White Christmas" played softly, and Jake was on one knee in the snow with a red velvet box open with a sparkling diamond in the slot.

Tears filled her eyes. "Jake!" She barely got his name out. Her heart was pumping hard like the little drummer boy was playing it.

"Lissy, I love you. Will you marry me?"

She handed Snickerdoodle off to her dad and rushed toward Jake, slipping on the fake snow, falling into his arms. Before he could get off his knees and prepare himself for impact, they both fell back. The group of their friends and family surrounded them, cheering. She grabbed his smiling face between her hands. "You remembered the snow."

"I did. But you didn't answer my question. Will you marry me?"

"Yes! Absolutely yes!" She kissed him, sealing the deal.

Turning her head, her dad holding Snickerdoodle, Andrea, Jenna, Susan, and Megan laughed and clapped. She and Jake got up, and she turned to her dad and Andrea. "You knew?"

"Yes, this young man has had this planned for some time. Andrea and I were always going to be coming home before today. We just pretended we weren't so I wouldn't accidentally spill the beans. You know I'm no good at keeping a secret." Her dad gave her a tight squeeze. "Congratulations, Sugarplum, you can finally live your high school dreams, no more scribbling his name in a notebook behind his back. You can proudly write Mrs. Jake Blessing anywhere you please."

"Dad!" She groaned, blushing.

Jake whispered, "You did that?"

Melissa nodded, her cheeks getting warmer and warmer. Jake seemed to puff up a bit and stand taller knowing that little tidbit, and she rested her head on his shoulder.

Frank handed Snickerdoodle back to Melissa and turned to Jake. "Welcome to the family."

Melissa clasped Jake's hand and gazed into his eyes. "I like the sound of that."

He brought her hand to his lips, kissed the top. "I do too." Then he petted Snickerdoodle on the head. "I'm going to be your new dad. I hope you're okay with that."

Snickerdoodle licked his hand, wiggling in excitement in Melissa's hands, trying to jump to Jake. He took her in his big hand, and she settled down.

"I believe that is a yes."

The happy couple laughed, leading the crowd into the cafe to celebrate their engagement and what was sure to be the most memorable Christmas ever in Cypressville.

The End

CHRISTMAS MISTLETOE BALL

KISSING BALL

In downtown Cypressville on Main Street, you will find SuSu's Petal Boutique, where the owner, Susan, makes mistletoe/kissing balls all year round. Within the first week of her grand opening, she sold out of her mistletoe balls when the tourists visiting their small town came for the Christmas festival. Over the years, Susan perfected making kissing balls for other events such as weddings or couples showers. She changed the holiday-themed holly, mistletoe, or pine to seasonal greenery and flowers on those occasions. Susan now keeps the shelves stocked year-round with an assortment of handmade arrangements. The size of each kissing ball varies from the starting base styrofoam sphere; Susan chooses anywhere from a small two-inch sphere to as large as a five-inch sphere for larger areas.

To learn how to make a mistletoe ball, follow these simple instructions.

YOU'LL NEED:
Styrofoam sphere of your choice

CHRISTMAS MISTLETOE BALL:

- 24 Gauge Wire | Or a cut piece of a straightened coat hanger wire
- Greenery | Holly, pine, or mistletoe
- 1/4 or 1/2 inch Ribbon | Max 38 inches long for hanging up

INSTRUCTIONS:

1. Stick the wire through the center of your foam ball until the end pokes out the bottom. Curve the tail end of the wire upwards towards the ball, so it hooks into the bottom. Press it in place. This ensures the ball will be secure when hung.
2. Strip the ends of your greenery and cut each sprig to your desired size, making sure they're all about the same length to create a uniform sphere.
3. Stick the stripped ends into the foam ball. Keep adding new greenery until your ball is as full as you'd like.
4. Bend the top wire into a loop, making a small circle. Tie a ribbon around the wire at the top of your Christmas kissing ball for added festive cheer.

Note: Keep mistletoe out of reach of children and pets, as the plant and berries are poisonous.

For more advanced instructions, a wide variety of instructional videos and articles are available online.

SNEAK PEEK

CHAPTER ONE

Jenna parked her car in front of her monogram shop and started walking toward the park. The early morning sun barely showed behind the clouds. Fog still hovered over the roads, waiting for the warmth of the morning sun to burn it off. She walked the quiet streets, a light mist brushed her skin. A breeze ruffled her dark bangs into her eyes. Jenna swiped them to the side, making a mental note to make an appointment to get them trimmed.

She was surprised when Melissa called her at five this morning and asked her to meet at the park so early. Her best friend rarely woke up before eight, so when she wanted to meet at six-thirty, Jenna jumped out of bed to get ready.

Jenna couldn't imagine what Melissa needed to talk about in person so early in the morning unless something happened with Jake. But why not come to her house? It made no sense. She bit her thumbnail, making up all sorts of issues in her mind as she passed by Susu's Petals, a cute boutique owned by Melissa's soon to-be sister-in-law.

Susan and her daughter, Megan, walked out of the shop as she passed by. "Morning, Jenna!"

Jenna stopped her progression and turned around to greet Susan. She dropped her concerned frown for Melissa, and she put on the bright expression she showed everyone and chirped, "Good morning!"

Megan ran up to Jenna and thrust open a bright purple umbrella shaped like a cute octopus, "Morning, Miss Jenna! Look at what I have."

"Wow! That's a super cool umbrella. I may need to get one."

Megan grabbed Jenna's hand and started tugging her back to the boutique. "You can. Momma sells them. They also have a big sunshine one. You need that one. It makes me think of you because it has a big smile on it just like you do."

Susan pulled her daughter back gently. "Jenna is going somewhere, Megs. She can come to the boutique later."

Megan pouted. "But I wanted her to see the umbrella."

Jenna squatted down and hugged Megan. "Aww, you are too sweet. I promise I will come back when I get a chance. When you get out of school, you can help me find it."

Megan cheered quickly, appeased, and started playing with her umbrella, opening and closing it.

Jenna stood back up and turned to Susan. "What are you guys doing out here so early?" She looked at her watch. It was almost six-thirty. "School doesn't start for another hour."

Susan answered, buttoning Megan's coat, "Jake asked us to meet him for breakfast at Main Street Java this morning. He wanted to talk to me and Megan about something important."

"Ooh, well, that is something," Jenna turned to Megan, thinking how strange it was that Melissa and her fiancé, Susan's brother, would both want to meet with them separately at the same time. "If it's good news, I hope you let me in on it."

Megan had the tip of the umbrella on the ground and was skipping around it. "Yeppers, I will." She stopped spinning and grabbed her mother's hand. "Come on, Momma. I see Lissy and Uncle Jake."

Jenna and Susan turned to where Megan was pointing. Jake kissed Melissa in front of Main Street Java before he went in, and Melissa started walking down the street to meet them. Susan let her daughter pull her away, laughing, and said over her shoulder, "See you later!"

Jenna smiled and waved. Melissa jogged the rest of the way to meet Jenna. She was smiling. So, Jenna's concerns were for nothing. Her curiosity was bursting now to figure out why Melissa called her so early.

Breathless, Melissa reached her. "Morning! Thanks for waking up so early to meet me."

They crossed the street and headed to the little park snuggled between two buildings. The park used to be an upholstery shop, but it burned down in the seventies. It had remained vacant for years until she and Mel were in seventh grade and the mayor back then had the whole town raise money to turn it into a park.

The two women sat on the park bench. Melissa pulled Snickerdoodle, her tiny Yorkie, out of her tote. The dog was dressed in a yellow raincoat and boots. Jenna laughed. "Oh my gosh, that has to be the most adorable outfit yet."

Melissa shifted Snickerdoodle to one hand, pulled out her phone, and handed it to Jenna. "Let's take a picture."

"What is that smile about?"

Mel held the dog up between the two girls' faces, and Jenna snapped the picture and handed Melissa back her phone. Melissa opened the image. "We all are wearing yellow.

If you had blonde hair instead of dark brown, we would all look related."

"Well," Jenna pointed to a little of Snickerdoodle's fur poking out of the hat. "We still could be, see. Her fur right here is starting to get a little darker."

Both women chuckled, and Melissa rubbed her puppy's head. Then, she hooked the leash on Snickerdoodle's collar and set her on the ground to roam about. "I think her big girl fur is going to be a little darker. Can you believe she is almost five months old?"

"Time flies."

"It sure does. Actually, that is one of the reasons I called so early. I was too excited to wait."

Jenna couldn't help but feel the excitement bouncing off Melissa and started to practically bounce in her seat. "What the heck is going on? I was so worried for a moment when you called so early. You never wake up before eight or nine. So, spill, I'm dying here."

Melissa squealed. "Jake and I set a date!"

Jenna grinned. "Finally, but why couldn't that wait?"

"Well, we just set it this morning. We stayed up all night talking. I haven't slept yet."

Jenna scooted closer to Melissa and hugged her. "I am so happy for you." When she sat back, she asked, "So when is the date?"

"June fourth."

Jenna looked at her fingers and counted. "Mel! That is only three months away."

"I know, but we don't want to wait anymore, and we started looking at houses online. We have a few appointments set up with the bank and a realtor. Jake's telling Susan and Megan now, but I wanted to talk to you alone because I have a huge favor to ask."

Jenna watched as Melissa's excitement turned to nerves

as she got up, wiped her palms on her jeans, and brought Snickerdoodle back to the bench. Jenna grabbed Mel's free hand. "Honey, you don't have to be worried; you're my best friend. I will do anything for you."

Melissa buried her face behind Snickerdoodle. "I'm not sure you're going to like this favor."

"Spit it out. You're making me nervous now."

"We'll it's really two favors. First, will you be my maid of honor?"

Jenna laughed. "Of course, I'd be honored! And what's the second favor?"

"I want you to design and make my wedding dress."

Jenna felt the color drain from her face. Since Christmas, Melissa was the only person in town who knew that Jenna inherited her uncle's skills at fashion design. Technically Jenna's family also knew she could sew, but she never told anyone that she had been making all of her own dresses and gowns for a while now. Melissa found out that the black dress she wore on her first date with Jake and the '50s-inspired dress she wore when the mayor married her dad last Christmas was Jenna's design. After that, Melissa kept insisting Jenna convert her shop into a store to sell her own clothes, but that idea was not something she could consider. Maybe in the past, but not now. Too many things changed.

Snickerdoodle's bark broke Jenna's train of thought. Melissa loosened her grip on her puppy. "Well? Will you? I mean, all the dresses you've made me and never told me or anyone were all amazing. I always thought your uncle sent them, but now that I know it was you, I can't think of any more memorable or special gift you could give me for my wedding. I think my mom would have been so proud of you."

Jenna wanted to cry. Melissa's mom had been like a second mom to her growing up, and she always used to buy her fabric scraps so Jenna could make barbie doll clothes.

Melissa's mom even had a sewing machine in the spare room for when they wanted to play design shop. So, the thought of Mel's mom not being there for her wedding, and the fact she probably would be proud made up Jenna's mind for her.

"Okay, I'll do it, but you have to swear to me that you won't tell a single soul besides Jake, of course, that I am making this dress. I can't have it out in the open. I'm not ready for that."

Melissa rushed to hug Jenna. "Thank you, you're the absolute best. I promise.

CHAPTER TWO

*J*enna closed her shop for a few days while she frantically drew designs and pulled fabrics, cutting silks and pinning pieces to a body form, trying to get ideas. With the date of the wedding so near, that didn't give Jenna much time to figure things out, and she had texted her Uncle Max to FaceTime her the moment he had some free time. Preferably before her lunch date with Melissa to discuss some final options.

After she had been working for nearly four hours straight, she texted him again, pleading with him to call her so he could help her figure out how to make the slip she'd pinned on the body form into what she drew. Finally, the phone rang.

She answered the phone without any greeting, instead, she cried out into the screen at her uncle's aged face. "This is a disaster!"

Through the video chat, her uncle Max furrowed his brow.

"Jenna, darling, turn the screen around and bring me closer to the dress."

"Max, there's no sense in showing you. It's not like you can fix it from New York over the phone."

"Darling, stop with the dramatics. That is my department. Now flip that phone around and let me have a look."

Jenna flipped the phone around and walked over to the beginnings of what would become a champagne-colored silk wedding gown. It was pinned to a body form crammed into the corner of her small sewing room in her monogram shop.

"Jenna, this is only the lining. I am sure whatever you design will look exquisite on Melissa. Now tell me what has you in tears."

She spun the phone around. "I'm not cut out for this. This dress is the first dress that I am making that will be on display and to make it more stressful, it's for my best friend's wedding." "And?" Max drew the word out.

Jenna plopped down on a tiny hot pink futon sofa across from her sewing machine and puffed. "And, I just found out Blair will be at the wedding."

Then after a few seconds of watching Jenna pout through the phone, he said, "Am I supposed to know who Blair is?"

"She's the girl who was all over social media last Christmas. Remember? I sent you the wedding of Melissa's dad that she livestreamed over YouTube."

Max's brows shot up and he whistled through his teeth. "Ah, yes, that video had over a hundred thousand views if I recall."

"Yep. Melissa, being Melissa, became friends with Blair strangely after she told her ex, Paul, that Blair was interested in him. Once they started dating, Blair started calling Mel for advice. Their entire friendship is weird, but now she is coming to the wedding. She will be judging me as the maid of honor and Mel's best friend and posting everything we do online. That alone is horrifying. I love seeing everyone, but I don't want to be in the spotlight. I don't want to be all over social media. It freaks me out knowing that someone out there might recognize me and come track me down."

"Honey, don't you think that you're being a little paranoid? I don't think a little social media here and there will bring stalkers to your door. You lived in the city with me for a couple of years and weren't this afraid. What's this really about?"

Jenna slumped in her seat and bit her thumbnail.

"Stop that."

Jenna removed her nail from her mouth and gripped the phone with both hands. She rested her elbows on her knees, face close to the screen. She spoke softly as if about to tell Max a secret. "Okay, I'll spill. I'm worried once Blair sees the dress, she'll want to know all about the designer. When she finds out this, *nobody*—" Jenna sat up and pointed to herself "—from

Cypressville designed it, the wedding will be roasted all over the internet. So, I will humiliate Melissa in front of all of Blair's social media following."

Max huffed over the phone.

"Don't roll your eyes, Max. I'm serious. Since Melissa planned the best Christmas festival our town has ever seen, social media took to it like flies to honey. I mean, I'm grateful and all because our economy skyrocketed, and the traffic of visitors coming in and out has been incredible. But I'm freaking out. What if—" Jenna cut herself off. She watched her own eyes widen in the small box in the upper right corner of the phone screen as she almost told Max her secret. Wanting to hide the expression, she turned her head, looking at the body form holding the pinned-up slip. She continued in the same hushed tones.

"What if whoever is watching and following Blair's vlogs only sees me as Jenna, the town blabbermouth, and tote bag monogram girl, a nobody, trying to play designer. This is too important. I don't want to be a laughingstock and ruin Melissa's wedding or her new business."

Max took a deep breath. Jenna turned to watch him, and her stomach twisted in knots as he stared silently and intensely at her through the phone, trying to read her. Her eyes started to burn, the rims filled with tears. She had a feeling he knew—

Max tutted and finally spoke. "What does Melissa say to all of this nonsense you're spouting?"

Jenna took a deep breath, relieved, then turned away from the phone, blinking her eyes a few times to stop the tears from falling and keep herself from spilling her guts even further. Her shoulders slumped slightly in relief, but then she sat up straight and told Max what he needed to hear. "Melissa is a sweetheart. She'd never be honest."

Exasperated, Max asked, "Darling, what did she say?"

Grudgingly Jenna answered with half-truths. She hadn't told Melissa anything. "She always thinks I'm being silly, but Max, Melissa practically wears a capsule wardrobe all the time. She doesn't know better, the only stylish clothes she wears are the things you send me that don't quite fit right, or I give to her."

"I think Melissa is one smart woman giving you this chance. One thing I did see in that Christmas video was the beautiful dress she wore at the wedding. Who designed that?" he asked with a smirk and a raised brow.

"Hush, Max. She thought you sent that to her until you acted surprised about how well it turned out and fit her perfectly. In fact, my being in this predicament is your fault. She fussed at me for almost two weeks that I had hidden this talent from her and lied about all the dresses I made her."

Max laughed heartily. "My girl, you certainly are an enigma. I'm glad Melissa found out. It's about time someone else sees your ability for what it is, pure genius."

Jenna felt her cheeks redden at her uncle's compliment.

"Honestly, I am surprised she hadn't figured it out earlier. I mean, you've been making things for yourself and drawing countless designs and patterns since you were both children. You even made all of your Barbie doll clothes. She had to know you were under my wing here in the city after high school. I find it hard to believe you've kept your talents hidden from your family and dear friends. Child, I know it's in your blood, you are my niece, after all, and I know you love it because, for the past eight years, you've tried to send me designs under fake names."

Jenna interrupted, shocked. "I nev—"

"Don't deny it, child." He held up his hand to the screen. Jenna bit her tongue as he carried on. "I'd know your designs anywhere. Just because you tried to be sneaky doesn't hide the fact that even you know deep inside, you have a gift. It disappoints me that you still have such low confidence."

Jenna wanted to argue it wasn't all low confidence but fear of being discovered and having her face plastered every-where. She screwed up years ago and was afraid of being found and having to fess up to her past childishness that had brought her back home to pick up the pieces. Not even Max knew the real reason for her fears.

"Darling, I have been telling you that you are a diamond in the rough for years. It's time to believe in yourself and shine." Jenna groaned.

Max ignored her. "Text me the design for the dress."

Without a word, she swiped the chat app up to go to her photo album app. Finding the design, she texted it to her uncle then reopened the chat app. "I just sent it."

Max's phone dinged. His face disappeared, leaving a black screen with pause typed in the center. Jenna bit her thumbnail, brow scrunched in worry as her uncle reviewed her design.

His face came back into view a minute later, expressionless. "Your design is classic with a twist of whimsy. Seductive, yet innocent. Very unique."

Jenna's stomach twisted into knots. "What does that even mean?"

"Darling, stop your worries. That was a compliment. This design is something many women today would want, I assure you. I could easily see your designs paired with the tuxes I design."

Jenna sank back into her seat, relieved that he didn't rip her design apart like he did when she worked with him back in New York.

"You have to say nice things to me because you trained me years ago." She glanced at the dress hanging on the body form,

disappointed. "I sadly know the truth."

Max rolled his eyes again. "Child, this is ridiculous."

He walked over to his window, his video shaking with each step. Jenna could hear the traffic through the phone. He sighed. "It's been a very long time since I've been home. Things here are practically running themselves with all of my assistants. Would it make you feel better if I came down there for support?"

Jenna stared at the phone for several seconds in shock. Then, finally, she sat up straighter and started to bounce in her seat. "Oh my gosh, you are brilliant. Yes, please come into town. That way, whenever Blair comes, she can meet you, and you can pretend to be the designer. I mean, you are well known all over the world. Melissa's wedding will go down in history as another win, and you will bring in more tourists just by being here if Blair posts about you."

She took a deep breath and rushed out, "Please, Uncle

Max." Jenna batted her eyes and gave her uncle her best puppy dog face. "I won't feel so stressed if you're here, and the attention won't be on me anymore. You know how I am. And I know with you here this dress will end up magazine-worthy."

Max made a noncommittal noise as he stroked his fingers in his long white beard, which had started trending on social media this past year. Since growing it, he'd been noted in some articles as the classy Saint Nick of fashion. Uncle Max, also known as Maximilian Thorne, was one of the top designers in men's fashion and had recently taken to modeling his creations. His suits and tuxedos were worn by more stars than Jenna could count, and sometimes while talking to her uncle, she forgot he was famous. Funny how when she lived in New York, she tried to hide the fact she knew him, and now she wanted to exploit him.

Thinking back on his offer to come to Cypressville she wondered what gave him a change of heart. She couldn't remember a time when he'd come home. In the past, he pointblank refused and would instead send money for her and her family to visit him in New York.

"Well? Will you come?"

"Darling, I don't think it's a good idea for me to take credit for your designs. You worked hard on them. It's time to own them. Plus, if they hit social media as if I designed them, I will have women pestering me to design their gowns, and you know I don't swing that way. I much prefer the male clientele."

Was that a no? Was it an impulse offer? Is this his way of getting out of coming? "Please, I need you, Max. I never asked for anything, even when I followed you around as your assistant for years. I learned everything you threw at me, did everything you asked, but I'm asking now. Will you please come and save me?"

"Didn't I save you once before when you cried for weeks on end over here and decided you wanted to go home? And once home, your parents had to call me after you arrived because you were in a depressed state for months. Not much I could do from over here, but if I recall, I had to practically pressure you into some sort of career, and I even bought you the building for your monogram shop."

"Ugh, alright, you don't have to rub that in my face."

"I'm not trying to rub anything in your face. I'm not exactly sure what happened back then, and I am not going to ask because I know that whoever hurt you made you miserable, and I know that feeling very well."

Jenna looked at her uncle over the phone. "How did you know I was having a hard time with a breakup?"

Max had an age-old sad look in his eyes. "Because I see that look in my eyes when I think of going back to Cypressville."

Jenna gasped. "Is that why you never come home? Tell me who hurt you, and I will tell you if they are still here. Maybe you've been staying away for nothing and —"

"No, he is still there, and I am the one who hurt him. I've seen him on Instagram. I followed the group of influencers who were there at Christmas."

"Max, I'm so sorry. You don't have to come home. I will manage."

"I know you will manage because I taught you everything you know, and you have the innate skill and a sharp eye. But I think maybe it's time I leave the past in the past and come home. I've been missing my roots as I age, and at seventy, I feel like it's time to reconcile my loose ends."

A moment of fear traveled through Jenna. Even though she called Max her uncle, he was more like her grandpa. He is her dad's uncle and basically raised her dad when his father died. "Loose ends, what do you mean? Are you sick?"

Max laughed. "Goodness no! I just meant that as you age, you start ruminating on your past and the what-ifs. I could have done things differently. Times were different in small Southern towns, and I wasn't ready to fight the fight. I think it's time I made amends."

Jenna melted into her sofa. Then, finally, she brought the phone back up to her face. "Thank goodness you are well, but now I'm curious. Who's the mystery man that stole your heart?"

He gave Jenna a mischievous smirk and his eyes twinkled as he brought his phone closer to his face, as if he were about to tell her. "That's for me to know and you to find out."

A door opening and the chatter of people could be heard coming from the background on Max's end of the call. He turned his head and said something to someone. "Sorry, darling, I need to go. I'll text you when I can make it into town. I'm hoping to tie up a few projects by the weekend. Then I believe I will be onwards to Cypressville."

He took a deep breath, closed his eyes for a moment. When he opened them again to the noise in his office increasing, he hurriedly blew Jenna a few kisses, and she returned them as she pressed "end." She threw the phone on the sofa cushion beside her. She slumped into the seat and grabbed a throw pillow, hugging it to her chest as she sighed in relief. Uncle Max would give her the courage and strength to finish Melissa's dress, and she would hopefully let everyone except Melissa and Jake believe he was the designer.

CHAPTER THREE

Ben walked through the garage door, entering the kitchen of the two-story, Colonial-style home in Metairie, Louisiana, where he grew up. His mom swayed to a soft classic rock song while scooping up the fresh-cut fruit and transferring it to a bowl. She hadn't heard him enter.

A wicked grin spread across his lips as he snuck up behind her, and put his hands on her shoulders. Startled, she yelped and squirmed away from him as she threw a handful of fruit in the air.

"Benjamin James Sanderson, you gave me a fright!"

He laughed as he picked up a pineapple chunk from the counter and popped it into his mouth. "Morning, Umma."

His mom picked up a towel and wiped her hands, then wound it and swatted him, aiming at his thigh. He scooted back, but the snap of the tip still got him.

He rubbed the sting out. "Dang Umma, that smarts."

"It should. It's not like I didn't do it enough to you growing up. Always making mischief, trying to overstep the line." She handed him the towel.

"Now help me clean up the mess before your father comes in.

With what you are going to approach him with this morning, we don't need to put him in a mood."

Ben's father loved order. As a disabled Marine sergeant, he ran his house and business in perfect order. When he lost his leg during the Gulf War, he had to learn to build his life up again and create a new routine. Then eight years ago, he had a massive heart attack and felt like his body let him down. The military paid for therapy for the entire family. The new adjustment had been hard for them all.

Since then, Ben's dad never wanted to travel anymore, made Ben work like a dog, and none of them ever got to go back to Korea to visit his grandparents and extended family. Ben missed it, he knew his mom did too, but she never complained. That was one of the reasons he worked so hard. He wanted to make sure that he and his dad made enough money to always have his grandparents flown in twice a year. But lately, his grandparents didn't want to travel either. It was like everything was changing, urging him to get his dad to change too.

It was time.

Ben started to pick up the fallen fruit from the floor and place it in the garbage disposal. He often thought about what direction his life would have taken if his dad had never had a heart attack and if he hadn't left his last semester at NYU to move home and help out. After a year of his dad's recovery, Ben moved back to Manhattan, got a job, and searched all his old haunts for the strange girl he met his last semester there who wouldn't give him her last name or address. But after six months, his dad fell ill again, and he had to move back home.

She was beautiful, intelligent, and creative, and Ben still dreamed about her. Besides her lack of personal information, they had so many things in common. None of the other women that he dated made him feel the way he had when they were together.

Ben sighed, trying to shake her from his thoughts. He couldn't understand why it got harder and harder each year rather than easier. Didn't time heal all wounds? Obviously not. His dad was a prime example of a man who struggled to heal from change.

This time of year always was more difficult for his entire family. It reminded them all of when life changed, but it reminded Ben mostly of his greatest regret. It was a beautiful, sunny spring morning when Ben met her in Central Park for coffee before class. She had been on a blanket leaning back on her hands, her head tilted toward the sun, her long black hair touching the ground. He had bent over her, casting a shadow over her face, and she opened one of her light green eyes at him. A grin and a giggle escaped her lips.

He leaned down to kiss her, and as they broke apart, he handed her the caramel mocha he had brought. She was the first person he'd met who loved coffee as much as he did.

That night he had big plans. Ben had invited her to dinner at her favorite restaurant. He hoped by expressing his love, he'd convince her to trust him with her last name and finally give him her phone number since he'd be going back home for the summer. They had been meeting up every morning at the coffee house for four months, planning each date before leaving the last one. He'd been patient playing by her rules, but that night he was ready to pull the information out of her.

Hours after they made plans, he got the call. His dad had a heart attack, and he hurriedly packed up to leave. He never made it back to New York. His roommate had to pack the rest of his belongings and ship them to him.

She was in his past. He'd never see her again. His therapist told him the reason he still thought about her so often was that he genuinely cared for the girl, and he carried guilt for leaving without a trace, along with regrets for respecting her wishes in playing along with her game and not getting her phone number.

His mom knocked his shoulder with hers. "Ben, hun, it will be alright. Dad's moods have been better lately. I honestly think this may be good for him. You need a break, and he needs to learn by working full-time for a while that it's time for him to retire and for us to travel. I'll have your back."

Ben hugged his mom. "Love you," he whispered into her perfectly coiffed hair. "Umma, don't you worry about me. I'm willing to put up with Dad's mood. Dr. Ledinsky was at the office with Dad after golf, and I overheard him tell Dad again it's time for him to let the reins go and retire. I am finally at the point where I won't continue working with him." After almost losing one of his best editors, who also happened to be his best friend, he had a wake-up call. Dad fumed for weeks after Ben overrode his acceptance of Jake Blessing's resignation, but keeping Jake working remotely had given him the most amazing plans for the future of Sanderson Press. It could save them this fiscal quarter.

"Actually—"

"Benjamin."

Ben stiffened at his dad's voice coming from behind him. He turned around. Ben's father, Jonathan Sanderson, stood in the entryway from the dining area to the kitchen, arms crossed, eyes cold and squinting, and all burly six-foot-four, intimidating as hell. The fact that he couldn't look down on Ben any longer took away the fear his dad used to inflict on him as a kid, but not the look of disappointment that always seemed to linger behind his dad's eyes these past few months.

Ben's heart clenched, and his stomach soured, but he hid the sadness that disappointment caused him. Instead, he mimicked his dad's stance. "Morning, Dad."

"Son." His dad nodded then looked beyond him, giving his wife one of his pointed stares. "Joon."

Joon passed by them with the bowl of fruit. As she passed her husband, Ben heard her whisper, "Be nice." She led the way into the dining area. "Boys, let's eat breakfast. You can talk over the meal."

Joon puckered her lips and knocked her husband on the arm with her elbow, making smooching sounds until Jonathan visibly relaxed. Ben's dad bent down so his wife could kiss his cheek and a soft smile crept onto his lips. Ben's parents didn't lack love, and his mom could always ease the tension from his dad's face.

Within seconds the entire energy in the room changed. Ben relaxed.

"Your umma's right. Let's talk over breakfast."

Ben and his dad grabbed a plate as his mom returned to the kitchen to grab the coffee carafe and the orange juice.

After they all started eating, Jonathan broke the silence. "What is it that you wanted to talk about?"

"Dad, I overheard Dr. Ledinsky and you talking the other day."

His dad served himself some eggs and bacon. "I'm not retiring if that's what you're aiming at."

Ben looked at his mom sitting across from him, serving herself. She made a slight nod.

"I wanted to talk to you about the next fiscal quarter."

His dad's right brow shot up. He put his fork down and turned toward Ben. "What about it?"

"Dad, you can't deny the numbers of the last two quarters. Sanderson Press needs to make some changes if we are to stay open. More and more new authors are self-publishing and working with the new print-on-demand machine to print their books. When we had to retire our old, outdated printing press years ago….” He trailed off, assessing his dad's reactions. Jonathan was still sensitive over the fact that his health and medical bills interfered with his ability to maintain the bindery. Ben had always felt guilty that he couldn't keep it running properly and felt his father blamed him for its disrepair. His dad scowled. When he didn't comment, Ben continued, “We took a huge financial hit when we shut down our bindery and began outsourcing.”

Jonathan grunted and nodded. Ben, slightly encouraged, continued. “When Jake went remote, it gave me an idea how to cut costs without compromising the quality of customer service you founded this company on and bring back the press.”

Jonathan hadn't moved, but he lifted his brows slightly. Ben had his attention. His dad had hated having to stop printing when the machine cost more to repair than print. Ben took a deep breath.

“I talked to a realtor a few days ago.”

Jonathan shifted and crossed his arms over his chest. “And, why would you need a realtor? Are you selling your house?”

“Well, not quite. I got them to look at our building.”

His dad slammed his hand on the table. “No! Absolutely not!”

“Dad, we're using less than half the space. It takes up more than half of our income to pay the costs to keep it up and running. If we sell, we can get a smaller space and have our employees work remotely. We could implement savings and utilize independent contractors as we grow and the need arises.

It's something to consider.”

"No! Absolutely not."

"Then I'm done. I can't work like this anymore. I'm exhausted trying to keep us above water. You have to see that Sanderson Press will soon be bankrupt if we don't do something to make changes."

"Benjamin, the subject is closed. You are the CEO and will not abandon your station."

"Dad!" Ben practically shouted.

His dad sat erect in his chair, glaring at him.

Joon quickly stood up and walked behind Ben's dad, placing her hands on his shoulders. She leaned down and gave her husband a quick kiss on his cheek. His mom knew his dad's love language well.

While she gently massaged Jonathan's shoulders, she changed the topic. "Benjamin, isn't Jake getting married soon?"

Instant relief engulfed the room. "Yes, in a few months."

His mom turned to his dad. "Jonathan, why don't you give Benny the next three months off until after Jake's wedding. That way, he can have a much-needed vacation, and you can see to the company. Then, talk to James in accounting and have him show you the books and think about what Ben has told you. It will be good for you both."

His dad was about to remark, but his mom placed her finger over Jonathan's lips. "You've taken Benny for granted lately. He's been walking in your shadow long enough. It's time you go back to work full-time instead of just sitting in your office to get out of the house. Maybe working full days for three months will remind you of why I am ready for you to retire."

Ben turned to his mom, gave her a crooked smile, and hope filled his eyes. She was an angel. Even though she rarely questioned her husband's ideals or interfered in business, she did have a way of making his dad listen to her. Ben waited patiently for his dad to process her words and respond.

"Your mother may have a point. She has been getting on to me about retiring for a while now." Jonathan glanced at Joon then Ben. The air seemed to let out of his body, relaxing his stern posture for only a moment before he sat straight once more. For the first time in years, Ben saw resignation in his dad's eye. Jonathan sighed, concentrated on eating a bite of fruit, and after a few seconds he said, "You haven't had a day off in practically eight years. I shouldn't have neglected to offer you time off. Every good man needs a break, and you are a good man, Ben. Take the three months off, and after your friend is married, we can revisit this discussion."

Ben opened and closed his mouth a few times, not knowing what to say. He honestly wasn't expecting the time off or that his dad would possibly agree. He was still upset that Ben renegotiated Jake's resignation and offered him more money and a contract position to keep him at the company because he was his friend. But it wasn't all nepotism. Jake was the best editor in the South East Region and he'd be a fool to lose him without a fight. Ben had truly mentally prepared for more arguments and was grateful it went so well. The rest of breakfast was less tense and almost enjoyable with his umma's change of topic to Jake's wedding.

When Ben opened the doors to the large building that housed Sanderson Press, the excitement started to sink in that he was finally able to get away for a holiday. Jenna crept into his mind. He wished she would leave him alone, but that woman and all of his regrets about how he left would haunt him for the rest of his life. Maybe a vacation and spending three months in Cypressville with Jake would get her out of his mind.

Thank you for reading the sneak peak of Love by Design. To find out the rest of Jenna and Ben's story, you can find the link on kristentassin.com or scan the QR code below.

A MOMENT OF YOUR TIME

Enjoyed this book? Please leave a review!

Reviews help indie authors like me reach new readers and help new readers decide if a book is for them.

Please take a moment to write a short review.

Thank you! Your support means the world to me, and I'm truly grateful for your time and feedback. Click HERE or scan the QR code below to leave a sentence or two.

BOOK EXTRAS!

Visit my website, where you can find extra goodies, such as images of the city, the cast, and merchandise for all my books and series.

https://kristentassin.com/cypressville

To stay in touch and be the first to find out about big news, book series, and giveaways, sign up for my newsletter at www.kristentassin.com. As an incentive, you will receive my first book ever written, a FREE Christmas in Cypressville ebook.

ACKNOWLEDGMENTS

To Karri and Tina, thank you for always being there to support, encourage, promote, and keep me focused on the end goal. Your time and support mean the world to me. To my sister Bernie, my first reader, knowing you loved this book every step of the way gave me hope that others would find the same kind of happiness you did. To my two beautiful daughters who believed in me even when I didn't believe in myself. You both mean the world to me, and I appreciate your love, loyalty, and ever-present support always. To Elizabeth, my best friend and chosen sister, thank you for helping to develop my imagination my entire life. And lastly, thank you to my critique group, whose opinions, time, and friendship helped bring out the best in me and my writing skills.

You all are the absolute best 

Kristen Tassin is an independent author whose lifelong passion for storytelling ignited into a full-fledged career. Overcoming the challenges of dysgraphia, she dedicated years to honing her craft while balancing motherhood and a demanding career. A hopeless romantic at heart, Kristen has always believed in the power of happily ever afters. Her southern roots and love for cozy winter vibes provide the perfect backdrop for her writing.

With a diverse background as a single mother, cosmetologist, and mental health advocate, Kristen infuses her stories with authenticity and depth. Her experiences interacting with people from all walks of life have shaped her ability to create compelling characters and captivating worlds.

Kristen's writing explores a range of genres, from the heartwarming charm of small-town romances to the enchanting realms of fantasy. Her dedication to mental health representation shines through in her work, offering readers relatable and empowering narratives.

Keep in touch, sign up for my newsletter at www.kristentassin.com

facebook.com/author.kristentassin

instagram.com/kristentassin.author

tiktok.com/@kristentassin.author

amazon.com/author/kristentassin

ALSO BY KRISTEN TASSIN

www.ingramcontent.com/pod-product-compliance
Lightning Source LLC
Chambersburg PA
CBHW020323160726
47992CB00004B/1669